shake it off

Also by Suzanne Nelson

shake it
off

Suzanne Nelson

SCHOLASTIC INC.

Copyright © 2019 by Suzanne Nelson

All rights reserved. Published by Scholastic Inc., *Publishers since 1920*. SCHOLASTIC and associated logos are trademarks and/or registered trademarks of Scholastic Inc.

The publisher does not have any control over and does not assume any responsibility for author or third-party websites or their content.

No part of this publication may be reproduced, stored in a retrieval system, or transmitted in any form or by any means, electronic, mechanical, photocopying, recording, or otherwise, without written permission of the publisher. For information regarding permission, write to Scholastic Inc., Attention: Permissions Department, 557 Broadway, New York, NY 10012.

This book is a work of fiction. Names, characters, places, and incidents are either the product of the author's imagination or are used fictitiously, and any resemblance to actual persons, living or dead, business establishments, events, or locales is entirely coincidental.

ISBN 978-1-338-33929-1

10 9 8 7 6 5 4 3 2   19 20 21 22 23

Printed in U.S.A. 40
First printing 2019

Book design by Jennifer Rinaldi

For Aimee Friedman, Olivia Valcarce, Jennifer Rinaldi, and the incredible team at Scholastic, in thanks for your talents and your fabulous foodie enthusiasm.

—SN

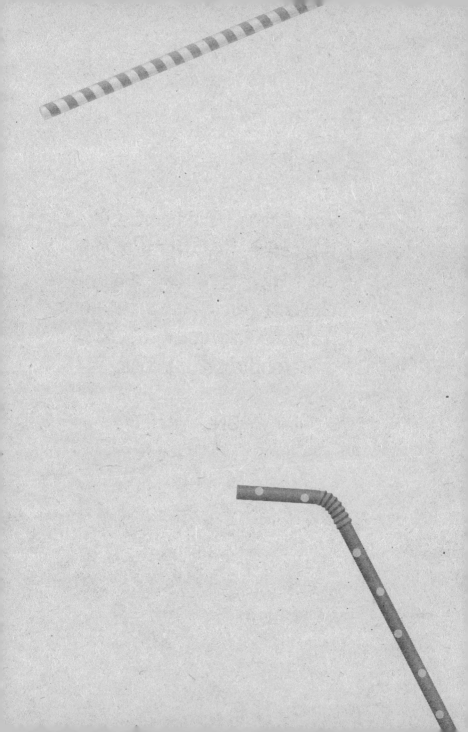

Chapter One

"It's over," I moaned as I collapsed into the booth across from my best friend, Leila. Even the sugary aroma wafting from the milkshakes behind the Sip & Shake counter—one of the best scents in the entire world—couldn't cheer me today. My spirits sank even further when I realized that Leila, her thumbs flying over her smartphone screen, hadn't even glanced up. Not that I could blame her. If I had *my* phone with me, I'd be doing the exact same thing right now.

I was still reeling from the fact that Mom and Dad had taken away my phone privileges for the *entire* summer.

I tried again, louder this time. "I said . . . It's. Over."

"Huh?" Leila's eyes flicked to my face, then back to her screen. "Oh. You mean your life?" She shrugged. "Yeah . . . it's over for sure."

Her nonchalant tone made my stomach clench. I wanted her to be as upset as I was. We were about to be separated for the whole summer. But she didn't look very upset. She looked as smilingly pretty and put together as always. Her enviable golden-bronze skin—so glowing compared to my own pale complexion—shimmered with the blush her parents let her use, and her sunflower-yellow maxi dress (which I'd picked out) made her look older and more sophisticated than any other soon-to-be seventh grader I knew.

"But, hey," she continued, "I ordered your fave, the Purple Pixie Dust. On me as a parting gift."

The Purple Pixie wasn't actually my favorite. All the towering milkshakes at Sip & Shake were amazing, but my favorite was the Heavenly Heath Cheesequake: a dulce de leche milkshake with bits of crumbled Heath bar and caramel cheesecake topping. I didn't correct her, though. Nobody ever corrected Leila Flores.

"Thanks. I have to drink quickly, though. I can only stay for a little while."

She rolled her eyes. "Right. I forgot. The whole forbidden friendship thing."

"Not forbidden." I shifted uncomfortably in my seat. "More like . . . discouraged." My parents didn't know I was meeting Leila here after school. They hadn't exactly *told* me I wasn't allowed to hang out with her. They'd said they were "worried about her influence" on me, and that I was "spending all my time with her." Then they'd told me the summer would be a "good break" from her. Leila, though, had been completely nonplussed when I'd confessed their critique to her.

"Parents are so pedestrian," she'd said. "They'll forget everything by next week. Mine always do."

I had my doubts about that. My dad is a seismologist and my mom is a professor of archaeology. Studying earthquakes and the demise of thousand-year-old civilizations seems to have fine-tuned their parental alert systems. They never forget *anything*.

"So where did you tell the 'rents you were going this afternoon?" Leila asked, her thumb swiping through her Instagram feed. I tried to see what she was "liking," but the pics were scrolling by too fast.

"To the library to return some books." I shrugged. "And I *am*. As soon as we're finished with our shakes."

She laughed. "Well, they can't punish you more than they already have. They took away your phone and they've exiled you for the whole summer. I mean, it's not like you cracked your screen on purpose."

"I know," I agreed. "I set it down on the locker room floor for two seconds and . . ." I cringed, remembering the ominous *Crunch!* when Sheena Jackson had stepped backward, right onto my phone.

"And two months away from Chicago?" Leila added. "It's like they're stranding you on Mars."

A car honked its horn, and I glanced out the window at the bustling street. Only a few blocks from my family's apartment and our middle school, Sip & Shake was the perfect hangout. I didn't just love the shakes; I loved that I could watch what felt like the entire world pass by outside the windows. Living in the main downtown area of the city, the Loop, felt like being at the center of a glittering galaxy of skyscrapers. Everywhere, there was something to see and do: light and people and beautiful noise. And I was about to lose it all.

I dropped my head into my hands. I wasn't leaving Chicago as punishment for breaking my phone, but that hardly mattered. It felt like the worst kind of punishment all the same. "Two months on a *farm*."

Leila's nose wrinkled, as if the very word summoned the smell of cows and chickens. "I still don't understand why your parents couldn't have just taken you to California with them. I mean . . . California or Iowa?" She raised her hands palms up and moved them up and down, as if she were a scale weighing the two options. "It's a no-brainer."

"I know." I sighed. "I begged them, but they're both going to be so busy with work." Dad was doing a hands-on field study of the San Andreas Fault, and Mom had agreed to teach at a summer program at Stanford University. They'd been waiting until I was old enough to make this trip, and this year they'd decided I was. "They thought it would be fun for me to visit the farm instead."

I couldn't admit the real reason Mom and Dad were sending me to my aunt and uncle's farm—especially not to Leila.

"Fun?" Leila smirked now. "Fun the way purgatory is fun."

"What am I going to do in small-town Iowa?" I hadn't visited my aunt, uncle, and cousins in years, but I remembered the musty smell of the farmhouse, the sour-milk scent of the creamery, and the flat fields of soybeans and corn that stretched for miles. The nearest town was at least a twenty-minute drive away.

"I don't know," Leila said. "My parents told me we might be passing through Omaha on a family road trip to Colorado this summer, and that was cringe-worthy enough. Iowa's way worse. At least your cousins are out there. What do they do for fun?"

I shrugged. "Last time I visited, I was seven. We played together. You know, swung on the tire swing. Swam in the creek—"

"Omigod. There's a tire swing? Is there an outdoor spigot, too, with one of those pump handles? Or better yet, an outhouse?" She giggled.

"It's not like that," I mumbled, my face heating.

Leila snapped her fingers. "Wait. I've got it. You could learn to knit . . . or crochet . . . whatever. And *then* create your own fashion line. Call it . . . Farm Chic. Or Manure Maven. Even better!"

She bent over laughing, and my stomach lurched. Manure Maven? But within seconds, I was laughing alongside Leila, playing it off as a great joke. Leila just had a sharp sense of humor, that was all. And even if her jokes were sometimes interpreted as digs by other kids at school, it hardly mattered. Because everyone—whether they understood her humor or not—appreciated her flawless beauty.

It was her amazing confidence that had made me want to be her friend from the moment she walked into the DeWitt Brayburn school six months ago. I'd figured it was a long shot; the most popular girls were soon vying for spots at her lunch table. I'd never really cared about popularity before. But then I'd been assigned as Leila's peer guide for her first few days at our school. I offered her a couple of my tried-and-true fashion tips—like how to pair one of her dad's slouchy sweaters with a chic skirt—and before I knew it, she was inviting *me* to join her at lunch.

"It's just until she gets to know people," I explained to my friends Devany and Jane, who I'd known since kindergarten.

Jane had been skeptical right from the start, as if she knew it was only a matter of time before I'd defect to Leila's lunch table for good. Leila just appreciated my fashion experimentations and obsession with *Project Runway* more than Dev and Jane did. Most mornings she FaceTimed me so I could choose her outfit and accessories for school. So I evolved away from Dev and Jane, or maybe we outgrew each other, until I was hanging out with Leila all the time, and only waving to the two of them when we passed in the hallways. Then the YouTube disaster had struck in May, and I'd barely spoken to them since then.

My face flushed at the memory of the YouTube video, but Leila, seeing my expression, misread the reason for it entirely.

"Come *on*, Bria. Get a handle on the sulking." Her voice was silk-smooth but commanding. "We just finished our last day of sixth grade! I didn't come here to be depressed. I came here . . ." She smiled when a waitress set down two titanic shakes in front of us. "For *this*." She swept a hand, beauty-vlogger style, around her frosted glass mug, which was coated with a layer of frozen ganache icing dotted with malt balls and sprinkles. Balanced atop the shake itself was a brownie covered with whipped cream and chocolate shavings, and sticking out of the brownie was a skewered chocolate-covered banana. "The Chocolicious Brownie Bonanza."

"Sorry. You're right." I mustered a smile as I peered down at my own shake, the Purple Pixie. There were three Pixy Stix jutting up from the blackberry-flavored shake, and a stack of blackberry and strawberry macarons stuck onto the straw. Purple sugar crystals dotted the pink icing that coated the top of the glass. It was mouth-watering, but something about the way it looked bothered me. The straw and Pixy Stix were too symmetrical, too perfectly balanced. I tilted the Pixy Stix, pointing them at three haphazard angles, and then slid the macarons off the straw and settled them into the mountain of whipped cream atop the shake.

"There." I sat back, pleased with the shake's new look. "Better."

Leila snorted. "I *am* going to miss your artistic eye." She sighed. "If only you could work that design magic on Heidi Brent's wardrobe."

Heidi was a frequent star on Leila's fashion-critique YouTube channel. I shook my head. "Now *that* would be a lost cause."

"There you go," Leila said appreciatively. "Way to overcome the funk."

I slid a spoonful of the shake into my mouth, and the tart sweetness of blackberries zinged pleasantly over my tongue. It wasn't Heath and cheesecake, but it was still delish. My spirits rose a bit. "I bet the summer will go fast, and before I know it, we'll be back here, getting more shakes." I took another bite. "In the meantime, we always have snail mail."

Leila grimaced. "Ugh. I'm getting a hand cramp just thinking about it." She shook her head. "Just nab one of your cousins' phones. Then you can text me whenever."

The next bite lodged in my throat. Did my cousins Wren and Luke even have phones? Last year when they'd come to Chicago for Thanksgiving, neither one of them did. Was I going to spend my summer in a social media black hole? No texting? *Nothing?!* It made me want to scream. I coughed instead. "I'm not sure that's—"

"If you want it badly enough, you'll make it happen." Leila's voice was no-nonsense. A second later, she guffawed into her shake and put her hand up to her mouth, whispering, "Heads up. Fashion disaster. Jane Woodard to your right. Pleated midi skirt with cropped flannel top."

I glanced over to where Jane stood in line to order. Since I'd known her, Jane had sported a bookish-grungy style that mirrored her love of reading and Pearl Jam. It was entirely unique to Jane, and I'd never had an issue with it before. But Leila thought Jane's patterns and colors clashed, and since she loved my style and hated Jane's, she had to be right.

Jane's eyes met mine for the briefest second, her mouth curling on the brink of a smile. Then she registered Leila in the booth across from me, and she instantly broke eye contact, her near-smile gone.

Jane had never brought up the YouTube video to me, and yet every time she looked at me, I caught a disapproval, or maybe sadness, in her eyes that made my throat a little tight.

Now I took in Jane's outfit, feeling Leila watching me.

I scoffed, then said in a low voice, "Disaster. Totally." My heart panged, then buoyed as Leila nodded her approval of my assessment.

"We are the fashion slayers!" She grinned and then, with her phone tucked under the table, snuck a pic of Jane's outfit.

Normally I would help her find the perfect headline to post with her video, but I looked down at the remains of my Purple Pixie instead. I'd promised my parents I wouldn't have anything to do with Leila's YouTube channel again. I hadn't told Leila that, though, and I wouldn't now, either. She'd only roll her eyes and make a comment about my parents' ridiculous rules. The rules *were* ridiculous, but I didn't want to lose any more privileges than I already had. Meeting Leila here had been risky enough. And that reminded me . . . "Hey, what time is it?"

Leila checked her phone. "A little after three thirty."

I stood up so fast I nearly knocked over my now-empty shake glass. "I've got to go! I told Mom I'd be back home by four and I haven't even gone to the library yet."

Leila sighed and stood up. "If we're going to stay best friends, you're going to need to get over this whole honesty thing. The less you tell the 'rents, the better. We'll have to work on that when you get back." I nodded, and she gave me a light-as-air hug. "Remember: Get your hands on a cell phone ASAP. I need the 'Bria eye' for summer clothes shopping." Then she sat down again, her focus already on her own phone once more.

"I'll see you soon!" My voice tried to rise cheerily but ended in an uncertain squawk. Leila didn't look up again, and neither did Jane when I tiptoed past where she was seated with her milkshake.

I stepped onto the sidewalk and into the throng of people. My parents were probably already packing the car for the drive to Iowa. By this time tomorrow, I'd be in the middle of nowhere, and I was so not ready.

Chapter Two

"Bria!" Mom's voice was chirpy with excitement, her hand nudging my knee. "Bria, wake up! We're almost there."

Groggily, I opened my eyes and looked out the car window. Looming in nightmarishly huge proportions was a dancing cartoon cow sipping a milkshake. The cow's googly eyes swirled around in her head, animated by some motor hidden behind the billboard she danced upon.

"That is *so* wrong." I grimaced. "That cow is basically a cannibal. Gross."

Mom giggled, her brown curls bouncing, as if being within a

few miles of her childhood home made her revert back to her five-year-old self. "That sign's been there for forty years. I love it."

I studied the billboard. Next to the cartoon cow, in bright pink letters, the sign read:

TURN HERE FOR DAWSON'S DAIRY AND CREAMERY.

HAYRIDES, CORN MAZE, MILKSHAKES, AND MORE!

IT'S *UDDERLY* DELIGHTFUL!

Aunt Beth and Uncle Troy could've come up with better advertising when they inherited the dairy farm after Grandpa's and Grandma's passing. But noooo. Aunt Beth had wanted to stay true to Grandpa's memory and left the sign unchanged. "Even the pun is tacky," I muttered.

Dad and Mom shot each other a meaningful "parenting" look, and I knew they were none too happy about my attitude. Which was fine by me, because I was none too happy about this entire arrangement.

"Come on, Ree-Ree," Mom tried. "The sign's endearing."

I sighed at Mom's use of my pet name. I'd never minded it until

Leila had spent ten minutes laughing about it when she'd come over to our apartment a few months ago.

"Ree-Ree? Seriously?" She'd been doubled over laughing. "What are you? Three?"

"Please don't call me Ree-Ree, Mom," I said now. "I'm not a baby."

Mom's shoulders stiffened, and she said softly, "Sorry. I keep forgetting you don't like it anymore."

I pulled my eyes away from the garish billboard to the flat green fields. The sunset sky was wide and unbroken, so expansive compared to the fragmented sky of Chicago. This sky was almost too immense; it gave me the sensation that I might get sucked up into its great, purpling vacuum and never be seen again.

We turned down the lane leading to the Dawson farm and creamery, and soon corn and soybean fields were replaced by fenced-in pastures full of grazing Holstein cows. Up ahead there was a white silo, low-lying whitewashed outbuildings, and the red house and creamery that made up the Dawson farm.

Panic and resentment washed over me. "I can't believe you're making me do this!" I burst out. "All because of that stupid YouTube video, which wasn't even my fault!"

"That's *not* why we're doing this," Dad said quietly. "Your aunt and uncle could use the extra help at the creamery. The Fourth of July is only a few weeks away, and they always plan a big event on the farm for it. But more than that . . . we *do* want you to use this time away from home to think about the choices you've made over the last year—"

"Leila's not a bad influence!" I shouted. "I've told you that a million times."

Mom sighed. She reached for my hand, but I yanked it away. "Bria. You've changed over the last year. You're starting to grow up, we know, but you haven't seemed like yourself."

"You don't know who I am. And if I've changed, it's for the better."

I waited for them to argue, but they were silent.

We pulled into the darkening parking lot of the creamery. I could make out a path of stepping stones that wound past the little restaurant, milking barns, silos, and a petting zoo populated by bleating goats. Beyond that was what looked like the beginnings of a corn maze.

Mom scrambled out of the car and went running (yes, *actually* running) toward the farmhouse behind the creamery, calling my aunt's name.

I glanced up at the red house. It was a half a century old and showed its age with weather-beaten wooden siding and warped windows. With its wraparound porch, hanging baskets of geraniums, and rocking chairs, it could almost be charming. But to me, it looked old-fashioned.

Dad offered me a fortifying hug. "Wren and Luke are probably so excited to see you."

I doubted that. At Thanksgiving last year, they didn't recognize the names of any of the plays and musicals I'd seen. Instead, they went on and on about a homecoming football game at their local high school, like it was the biggest thing since smartphones. The visit ended with us promising to keep in touch, but Wren and Luke had both looked visibly relieved as they climbed into their Chevy Suburban to head back to the farm.

"Bria!" I heard my aunt's voice before I saw her. Despite her petite frame, she burst from the farmhouse's door with the force of a tornado, and grabbed me in a fierce hug. "I swear, you've grown a foot since the last time I saw you!" She held me at arm's length, taking in my watermelon-pink espadrilles and lime-green sundress. I'd added one of Mom's vintage scarves as a belt for good measure. "My, my, you're all sophistication and style, aren't you?"

When I only shrugged nonchalantly, Mom said, "You should see the outfits she puts together. She was nominated for best dressed in her class this year."

I hadn't won. Leila had, which was no surprise. But what nobody except the two of us knew was how many times I'd picked out her outfits. When she'd won best dressed, she'd thanked me, saying, "I knew letting you be my friend would be worth my while."

"Well, Miss Fashionista," Aunt Beth said, "what do you think of our new creamery uniforms, then?" She proudly smoothed out her red polo shirt, which was emblazoned with the words "Cow Whisperer" across the front, and the Dawson's Dairy and Creamery logo on the pocket. "I have one for you, too! Aren't they hilarious?"

"Um . . . sure." I forced a smile. Oh, if I could only tell her what I really thought. It was so, so tempting. And there was no way I was putting on that shirt. Ever.

"Liar!" my cousin Wren said quietly as she appeared in the doorway, along with Uncle Troy. "You are so lying right now. The only person on the planet who thinks these shirts are hilarious is Mom, and that's only because her sense of humor has been warped by years of exposure to cow manure."

Aunt Beth clutched her chest and pretended to stagger in pain. "How could you say such a thing?" she moaned, but she was laughing.

Wren rolled her eyes at me. "Thank goodness you're here." She jerked her head toward Aunt Beth. "It's hard to handle all her cheesiness alone." She grinned, and I noticed that she looked taller, and older, than the last time I'd seen her. Even though Mom and Aunt Beth resembled each other, Wren and I looked nothing alike; Wren had dark brown, straight hair while mine was auburn and curly. My skin was pale and I sunburned easily while Wren's skin always got tan from being outside so much.

And, of course, our styles couldn't have been more different. Wren's hair was short—in a no muss, no fuss pixie cut—and her carpenter jeans and steel-toed work boots were caked in dried mud. Or at least, I *hoped* it was only mud (considering the accusation she'd made about her mother).

"I'd hug you, but . . ." Wren gestured to the dirt.

"Thanks," I said gratefully, but my relief only lasted a split second, because Uncle Troy swooped me into a bear hug that lifted me off my feet, and his clothes were in even worse shape than Wren's.

"Welcome to Dawson Boot Camp, niece!" boomed Uncle Troy, his ruddy, sun-freckled face beaming as he set me back on the ground. I glanced down at my dress to find it covered in dust. "Drills begin at zero five hundred tomorrow morning. Will you be ready?"

"Zero five hundred?" I racked my brain, trying to remember what that translated into. I'd nearly forgotten that Uncle Troy, a retired marine, always spoke in military time. Zero five hundred meant . . . five o'clock in the morning! "Ha!" I laughed. "Very funny, Uncle Troy."

I waited for somebody else to laugh at his joke, but nobody did. After a beat of silence, Aunt Beth told Wren, "Why don't you show Bria where to put her things while I catch up with your aunt and uncle? The boys will be back from the pasture in a few minutes, and then we'll all sit down to dinner."

I wondered who "the boys" were; wasn't it just my cousin Luke who was missing?

Wren nodded, scooping up my suitcases like they were light as feathers, even though I'd packed up my entire summer wardrobe, including every pair of shoes I owned.

As I scrambled to catch up with Wren, one of my espadrilles caught the edge of a stepping stone. With a cry, I barely saved myself from face-planting. Wren glanced down, saying matter-of-factly, "I hope you brought other shoes. You won't want to wear those around here."

It wasn't meant as a dig, only as a statement of truth. That was Wren's way. She'd always been quieter than me, but she wasn't shy. Her words were like her clothes: chosen for their practicality rather than their entertainment value.

"I brought other shoes," I said. "But not work boots."

"I might have a pair that'll fit you."

I looked at her boots. If they'd been Doc Martens, I could've appreciated them as iconic. But they weren't. "I'm not wearing those ugl—" I stopped, catching myself just as Wren leveled her eyes at me. She didn't seem angry, but she clearly wanted to see if I had the guts to finish my sentence. "I'll be fine with the shoes I brought," I said.

"Suit yourself."

Inside, the house smelled of old wood and cinnamon, and the floorboards protested with each step I took across the braided rugs. I remembered feeling very cozy among its chaos the last time I was here. Now I imagined what Leila would say: "Shabby but definitely *not* chic."

When I spotted a computer on a desk in the den, my spirits lifted. "You have internet, right?"

"Our Wi-Fi's sketchy," Wren said. "The signal on your phone might go in and out."

"I don't have a phone this summer," I said through gritted teeth.

Then, sensing an opportunity to get my hands on one, I said, "But you do, right?"

To my horror, Wren shook her head. "Luke has one, but I don't. My friends come by the creamery a lot." She shrugged. "You can't go anywhere around here without running into somebody you know, so a phone seems pretty pointless to me."

"But—but what about social media?" I sputtered, unable to believe what I was hearing. "Posting pics? Texting?"

"Not my thing," she said simply, and then turned for the stairs.

I felt my chances of being able to text Leila slip away as I dragged my feet upstairs after Wren. We passed the prehistoric bathroom, with its claw-footed bathtub and never-warm water (sigh), and dropped my suitcases in the bedroom we'd be sharing. Wren's bed was half-covered with 4-H magazines, open to articles on raising calves and innovations in milking machines. I took a quick peek at her closet and saw that I didn't need to worry about having enough room for my clothes. There was one simple chambray shirtdress; a plaid, belted tunic; and a half a dozen canvas work pants, dunga- rees, and jeans.

With a sinking heart, I followed Wren back down into the kitchen, which was full of Mom and Aunt Beth's laughter.

"There's the cuz!" Luke cried, grabbing me around the neck to give me a noogie, and ruining my meticulously tamed auburn hair. Luke looked a lot like Wren, only he was much taller and broader—and rowdier.

"Leave her be, you animal," Aunt Beth teased Luke. "You don't see Gabe doing that. At least one of you boys knows how to behave like a gentleman."

It was then that I noticed another boy standing in the kitchen. I tried and failed to press my flyaway curls back into place as he smiled at me. He had the most striking gray eyes I'd ever seen, an angular jaw, light brown skin, and tousled black curls. My heart gave a staccato beat. He was *beyond* cute.

The boy shot Luke a mocking look that seemed to say, *See? Your mom loves me best.*

Luke rolled his eyes. "Gabe, you're such a suck-up." He made a playful lunge at the other boy, nearly knocking half the dinner plates off the table in the process.

Uncle Troy tried to put a stop to the roughhousing while Wren and I sat down with my parents and Aunt Beth.

"You remember Gabriel Reeves, right?" Wren asked me. "Luke's best friend? He's in eighth grade, same as Luke." I shook my head (I was sure I would've remembered *any* boy as cute as he was).

"Gabe, this is my cousin Bria Muller," Luke explained as the boys finally took their seats along with Uncle Troy. Gabe smiled at me again, and my heart skipped another beat.

"Our families have known each other forever," Wren said, piling my plate with Aunt Beth's famous mashed potatoes. "He's helping out on the farm this summer."

"More than helping." Aunt Beth gave Gabe a proud smile. "He's the *real* cow whisperer around here."

"You know how some people are crazy about dogs or cats?" Wren said, passing me my plate. "Gabe's like that with all animals, but especially our cows."

Aunt Beth nodded. "I swear, he can read their minds."

I wrinkled my nose. "Why would anyone want to?" Mom gave

me a disappointed glance and the good humor that had infused the room cooled.

Gabe's smile dimmed a bit but didn't disappear. Instead, he tilted his head at me quizzically, as if trying to decide whether to take me seriously or not. In a quiet, steady voice, he said, "There's more to learn from a cow than you'd expect."

I snorted. Was he for real? I was about to ask him this very question when the phone rang, making everyone jump.

"Don't get it, Mom," Wren said, a sudden frown on her face. "You know it's the Vulture."

"Who?" my mom asked, giving Uncle Troy a questioning glance as Aunt Beth answered the phone.

"Hello, Mr. Brannigen," Aunt Beth said into the phone, her voice tight. "Yes, I got your email about stopping by to tour the facilities. Tomorrow? Well, I'm not sure—Yes, I'm aware you're considering other properties . . ."

Luke muttered something about a "bloodsucker" while Wren stuck out her tongue toward the phone.

Aunt Beth sighed. "Tomorrow will be fine," she said, and hung up the phone.

Uncle Troy, Luke, Wren, and Gabe all muttered "CheeseCo" in unison.

"What's CheeseCo?" I asked.

Luke looked at me in disbelief. "Only the biggest dairy production company in the country. That was their big-shot representative Mr. Brannigen, aka the Vulture. He's been calling for years, trying to get Mom and Dad to sell our land to CheeseCo so they can convert it into a branch of their dairy operations."

Worry streaked across Mom's face as Aunt Beth took the seat beside her again. "I didn't think you were seriously thinking about selling . . ."

Aunt Beth looked sheepish and Uncle Troy turned to Mom. "We're just giving them a tour, Lettie," he said. "Nothing's decided."

Silence settled over the table as we ate, and then Uncle Troy declared, "Enough CheeseCo for tonight." He smiled at me and my parents. "Let's kick off Bria's summer on a high note.

We'll clean up in here and watch some *Star Trek*." He clapped Luke on the shoulder and winked at Wren. "What do you say, troops?"

Gabe nodded. "Original series, right? William Shatner, best Captain Kirk ever."

I burst out laughing. "Vintage TV? You're kidding."

Gabe shook his head, looking amused. "What, do you prefer modern *Star Trek*?"

I opened my mouth to give a vehement *no*, but stopped when Dad stood up from the table.

"We'll have to skip it, I'm afraid," he announced. "Lettie and I should get back on the road."

I swallowed. *This was it.* Soon, we were all standing on the front porch saying goodbyes.

"We'll call every day," Dad said as he hugged me.

Mom beamed at me. "I love that you're getting to spend the summer the way I always did as a girl. You're so lucky to have this time here."

Lucky was not the word I'd been thinking.

She handed me a book-shaped package wrapped in teal paper. "This is for you." I tore it open to see a spiral-bound sketchbook with an illustration of a strawberry milkshake on the cover. "You have such an artistic eye, and you doodle on your school binders all the time. Maybe you could use this for drawings. To design some outfits? Or sketch other ideas?" Her voice scooped hopefully. "I left you something else, too. Inside your suitcase. Or . . . one of your suitcases." She gave me a meaningful look. "In case you need to reach out to a friend."

Yes! My heart leapt. She'd decided to leave me my phone after all. I threw myself at her, hugging her again. "Thanks, Mom!" Maybe I *would* survive the summer.

I waved as she and my dad climbed back into our car and drove away. Then I rushed back inside, taking the stairs to Wren's bedroom two at a time. I frantically unzipped first one suitcase, then the other, and then the last, shaking their contents onto the floor. But it wasn't my cell phone that fell out amid the heaps of shoes and clothes. It was a note.

With sinking spirits, I read:

Bria, always be brave enough to be you. Love, Mom

Written below that was Jane's mailing address, email, and home phone number.

"I don't believe it," I whispered. Jane was my *former* best friend, the one who I hadn't spoken to in over a month. Why would Mom do that?

I stared out the bedroom window and saw my parents' car—already a distant speck. I crinkled up the paper and threw it as hard as I could back into the suitcase.

There was a knock on the bedroom door, and Aunt Beth, Uncle Troy, and Wren peeked inside—all three hopeful, expectant.

"Ready for that Trekkie marathon?" Uncle Troy asked.

"Actually . . ." I faked a yawn. "I'm pretty wiped. I think I'll go to bed."

Puzzlement flicked over Aunt Beth's face, but she nodded. "All right, hon. Get a good night's sleep."

Uncle Troy smiled. "Briefing and boot camp in the morning."

"Dad! *Try* speaking civilian for once." Wren fake-glowered at him, and he rubbed her head playfully in response. "He means we'll give you a tour of the farm tomorrow." With a tiny smile, she followed my aunt and uncle back downstairs.

I brushed my teeth and changed for bed quickly, but once I was lying on the old mattress, half-sunken with age and squeaking with my smallest movement, I couldn't sleep. There was no AC, so every window was open to the night air. A chorus of crickets sang in the fields, with the occasional lowing of a cow. This night music was strange and foreign to me.

I closed my eyes, trying to call up the soundtrack of Chicago—the steady hum of traffic and rumble of delivery trucks over manholes; the occasional shout or laughter echoing through the streets; the muted classical music drifting through the walls of Mom and Dad's study as they wrapped up work for the night. I couldn't quite conjure the happy chaos of city sounds.

There was no doubt about it. My summer was over, and it hadn't even begun yet.

Chapter Three

I sat bolt upright in bed, on the verge of screaming as an alarm blared inches from my ears. What was happening? Adrenaline surged through me as I stared into the blackness of the strange room. Then a blinding light flicked on, and I couldn't decide if I should cover my eyes or my ears.

"Morning, sunshine," a voice deadpanned.

I squinted and saw Wren, already dressed in cargo pants and a worn gray T-shirt, shutting off the screeching alarm clock. In a flash, it all came back to me. I was in Iowa . . . on my aunt and uncle's farm. To make matters worse—I glanced at the clock and nearly screamed all over again—it was four forty-five in the morning!

"Wren, what are you *doing*?" My voice was raspy. I sank back against my pillow and pulled the covers over my head. "It's the middle of the night!"

Wren emitted her short *"Ha!"* then added, "This is the time we get up every day. The cows have to be milked and mucked first thing." She lifted a corner of my sheet, peering down at me. "Better get a move on or Dad will come in with ice water."

"Wha—?"

I couldn't even finish forming the question before Uncle Troy's overly cheerful voice boomed from the hallway. "There's nothing like a bracing ice shower to start the day off right!" Thankfully, I guess, instead of a freezing shower I got his floorboard-shaking rendition of "Oh, What a Beautiful Mornin'."

"It's official," I moaned. "I'm in purgatory."

"Nah." Wren grabbed her work boots from the closet and headed into the hallway. "Mom's corned beef hash is too good for purgatory. And if you don't get to breakfast in five, Luke and Gabe will eat every last bite of it."

She was right; when I stumbled blearily into the kitchen fifteen minutes later, breakfast was already finished and cleared away. Everyone had left for the barns, but it seemed that Wren had been tasked with waiting for me. She hopped up and handed me an egg sandwich. At least something was still left. She eyed my cute floral shorts and purple tank top.

"You won't want to wear that. Do you have any cargoes? Or jeans? Something that can get dirty?"

I *loved* this tank. I'd frayed the hem of it myself, and added some beaded fringe with fabric glue. It was one of a kind.

"I brought two pairs of jeans and some capris, but . . . will they get ruined?"

"Pretty much." Wren shrugged matter-of-factly. "I'll get you something to wear." She dragged me back upstairs and shoved a pair of dingy cargo pants and a ragged gray tee into my hands. "You can borrow these. You'll have to change into the creamery uniform after the barn chores are done anyway."

I took the clothes reluctantly. Well, I could at least knot the tee at the waist to make it a little less sad. "The thing is . . . I don't really do dirt," I said as I turned around to change.

Wren gave another short "Ha!" of a laugh and was soon dragging me back down the staircase once again. "Oh, it's more than dirt."

Worry prickled at me. "What do you mean, *more* than dirt?"

Wren didn't respond, and soon we stepped into the milking barn, where Luke was waiting for us—along with Gabe. When Gabe caught my eye, my adrenaline went haywire. He was looking way cuter than any boy should at five a.m. It flustered me so much that I almost tripped walking over to him.

Gabe smiled in amusement. "Not a morning person, huh?"

"This is *not* morning," I protested. "The moon's still out!"

"My favorite time of day," he said.

We would have to agree to disagree.

The barn was old but relatively clean, with only a slight tangy scent of milk to it. I thought I'd find manure all over, but not here—I supposed everything had to be kept as clean as possible to keep the fresh milk untainted.

The cows were lined up in two rows on a slightly elevated platform. Wren and Luke moved among them, prepping each of them with iodine disinfectant before attaching the tubes that would pump the milk from the cows into waiting sterile canisters.

"That is wrong on so many levels." I grimaced, watching the suctioning tubes. When I tried to avert my eyes, my gaze fell on an Iowa Beef Council sign hanging on the barn wall that read: EAT BEEF. THE WEST WASN'T WON ON SALAD.

"Eeew." The last bite of my breakfast sandwich lodged in my throat. "You eat your cows?"

"It's the *ciiiiircle* of farm life!" Luke sang theatrically until Wren swatted him.

Both of my cousins moved confidently around the cows, reaching underneath them without as much as a single flinch. Personally, I thought they were way too close to those hooves for comfort.

"Milking doesn't hurt the cows at all," Wren was saying to me. She ducked under one to attach the milker. "It mimics a calf nursing, and . . ." She straightened, giving the cow an affectionate pat as the milking machine quietly hummed to life. "It gives us all the cheese, milk, and ice cream for the creamery."

I closed my eyes, wishing I could click ruby heels together like Dorothy and be magically transported back to Chicago. I opened my eyes expectantly but—no such luck.

What I *did* see was Gabe holding a guitar and moving toward the line of cows. My knees weakened. Give a boy a guitar, and his cuteness increases tenfold. Everyone knows that.

Gabe sat down on an overturned bucket with the guitar on his knee. "Okay, who needs a serenade this morning?"

Wren gave him one of her rare smiles and motioned to the two cows closest to him. "Matilda and Betsy. Matilda's being her usual moody self and won't let anyone near her but you."

"Come on." I looked at Wren and whispered, "He's not seriously going to play for the cows?"

"Sure," Wren said. "The music makes them milk better."

I stared, full of skepticism, as Gabe began strumming his guitar and talking to one of the cows. Betsy? Matilda? Who knew? He was talking to her softly, as if she were a child who needed soothing. Somehow, his gentleness was endearing, even if he *was* playing for a cow.

"You must really love these cows, don't you?" I asked Gabe when he was done playing.

"Absolutely." He smiled. "I wouldn't be working here if I didn't. My dad's a doctor, and he wanted me to help him out at his office this summer. But there was no way I was cooping myself inside a stuffy office when I had the chance to be here instead." He held out a pair of gloves and the blue canister of iodine solution toward me. "Are you ready to try? I can help if you need it."

"Not a chance." I waved away the gloves. "This is why I buy milk from a store. So I don't have to deal with . . . *this*." I gestured at the cows.

"Right. It's so much easier not to think about where it all comes from."

I stiffened. "Well, it's way more appetizing to live in denial."

He laughed. "You're going to be a tough sell on farm life, aren't you?" When I rolled my eyes, he gestured for me to follow him out of the barn. "Luke and Wren can finish up in here," he said. "Maybe you'll do better with the goats. They're real characters. They'll crack you up." He grabbed a shovel from the side of the barn and motioned for me to do the same. "Come on. I'll help you muck out their pen."

Before I had a chance to ask what he meant, Gabe was through the gate and wading through the sea of bleating goats. With my reservations growing by the second, I followed. As soon as I stepped inside the pen, the goats mobbed me, nibbling and nuzzling. One tawny goat with creepy light blue eyes pawed me with its front hooves like an overexcited puppy. I thought I might fall over.

"Get down!" I tried to shoo it away, but didn't want to touch it. "Off!"

"That's Tulip," Gabe said. "She's usually shy with new people. She likes you."

"Yeah, well. The feeling's not mutual."

I looked at Gabe, and saw that he seemed perfectly at ease around the goats. With his broad shoulders, rolled-up sleeves, and dust-coated jeans and boots, he had the rugged farm-boy look down. He interacted with the goats calmly and thoughtfully, whispering in their ears and stroking their sides.

And then . . . there was me.

I finally realized I would have to touch them eventually and pushed Tulip away, trying to ease around her. Undeterred, she followed me, bleating in a plaintive tone that definitely meant "pet me."

"Let's just get this mucking thing over with so I can get out of here before she hooves me to death."

Gabe smirked, clearly underestimating the goats. "So you want to look for goat pellets, scoop them up, and toss them in this bin here." He pointed to the little brown pellets—hundreds of them—littering the ground.

"That's *not* what I think it is. Is it?"

"Oh, it's goat manure, all right." A completely aggravating smile spread across his face.

I stared at the piles on the ground and was hit full force by the injustice of it all. Back in Chicago, Leila was probably still fast asleep. And what was *I* doing? Cleaning up goat droppings. It was too much.

"How's it going out here?" Wren asked from the fence railing.

"I am not a human pooper scooper." I propped my shovel against the gate. "I'm *not* cleaning that."

Gabe looked up from his own work, on the verge of a grin, as if he thought I was joking. When he saw I wasn't, he whistled under his breath, then glanced toward Wren. "The immersion therapy's not working," he declared.

"You think this is a joke?" I glared at him.

He shook his head, but he was still smiling. "Luke and I have to get the tractor ready for the hayrides." He maneuvered among the goats smoothly and, as he passed Wren on his way out, mumbled something that sounded like, "Good luck."

"Why don't you go change into your creamery uniform?" Wren said to me. "I'll finish up here." Her voice was clipped as she picked up my shovel. "The creamery opens at eleven, but we have a lot of prep work to do beforehand. I'll meet you over there in fifteen minutes. I think you'll have an easier time in there."

"Thank god," I muttered, picking my way through the goats huddled around my legs. Tulip gave my shirt a firm tug from behind, as if begging me to stay. "Sorry, Tulip, but you picked the wrong girl."

Fifteen minutes was enough time to change and call my parents. If they had any love for me at all, they'd turn the car around and come back for me. The sooner, the better.

I was still fuming from my phone confab with Mom and Dad when I got to the creamery, hours after I was supposed to. Of course they'd told me that I was stuck here for the summer (groan), and I better start getting used to it (double groan). Now I threw open the door to the creamery and stomped inside, looking for Wren.

I'd taken *slightly* longer than fifteen minutes—it was already almost lunchtime. There were a few customers scattered about the dining room, chatting over their burgers and milkshakes. There were also a lot of empty booths. And no wonder. With its clichéd red-and-white-checkered tablecloths, bland country-themed art, and the sort of vinyl-covered metal chairs you'd find in bingo halls and church basements, the creamery was nothing much to look at.

One group of girls about my age was sitting in the booth closest to the sales counter, chatting easily with Wren as she worked the register; they were obviously her friends. When they caught sight of me, they exchanged knowing looks with Wren, and I wondered what, exactly, she'd told them about me. But then, in classic Wren fashion, she answered the question for me.

"You're late," she said when I reached the sales counter. "We've been open for a half hour already. Summer lunchtime is our busiest rush."

Riiiight. That was what had her and her friends in a huff. "Well, it looks like you had it covered," I responded, not wanting to admit that the reason I was late was the nap I'd taken back at the house. (Again, four-forty-five wake up. I was entitled, wasn't I?)

I turned my attention to the menu displayed behind the counter. I expected to see several kinds of burgers, maybe a vegan or salmon burger option, and a salad menu. But there were only two food choices:

BURGER BASKET WITH FRIES

BURGER BASKET WITH ONION RINGS

Below that was the shake menu; I imagined all sorts of outlandish shakes like the ones I loved back home, but again, I was disappointed:

"That's it?" I said. "You don't have any other kinds of shakes?"

Wren laughed. "We're not a five-star gourmet restaurant. We're just a farm, and Mom and Dad like to keep things simple. There's always so much to do around here, we don't have time for fancy."

"That's so boring. You could do a lot more with shakes. There's this place in Chicago that my friends and I go to where they add all these crazy toppings, and—"

"Our customers are happy with how things are," Wren said abruptly as she snapped shut the register.

Her friends stood up to leave then, and she waved to them with a "See you guys later." Then she turned back to me. "This isn't Chicago. Not everything has to be trendy."

"It does if you want anybody to notice."

She gestured to her baggy cargoes and oversized creamery shirt. "Then, I guess I'm not 'on trend,' either. Oh well." Her tone was lightly sarcastic, but there was defensiveness to it, too, as if I'd just insulted her.

"I didn't mean you. I was talking about the creamery . . ."

"It's fine." She waved a dismissive hand. "I could give a goat pellet whether anybody thinks I'm trendy."

Aunt Beth poked her head out of the kitchen and saved us from our awkward silence. "How's everything going? Having a good day so far, Bria? I'll bet you're a pro at farm chores already." Her brown eyes lit with hopefulness.

"Not quite," I murmured.

"Don't you worry, honey. You'll get the hang of it." She clapped her hands definitively. "In the meantime, we'll give you a job in here that's nice and easy, okay?"

I opened my mouth to say I didn't want another job at all, but the words were lost in the sound of screeching brakes. Through the windows I could see a yellow bus pulling into the parking lot.

"Oh boy," Aunt Beth said. "Swarm of summer campers on the horizon." Then she disappeared back into the kitchen.

"We're about to get really busy," Wren warned. "Look. It's obvious you don't want to be here, but I'm going to need your help. I can't deliver food trays *and* cover the cash register. Can you handle making shakes and carrying trays to tables? I'll show you how to use our shake machine. It's pretty simple."

"Anything's got to be better than mucking" was my reluctant response.

But an hour later, *nothing* was better. The camp kids had mobbed the tables, and I'd been on my feet nonstop, rushing to and from the kitchen window to pick up and deliver burger baskets. I could feel blisters forming on my heels and toes in Wren's unfamiliar boots. There were mottled grease stains on my creamery shirt, and a chocolate stain on my skirt from where I'd spilled a shake earlier. I never knew waiting tables could be this hard. People ordered fries when they meant onion rings, or vice versa, or they complained about how long the food was taking, and then told me it was *my* fault.

"This is the most thankless job ever," I complained as I limped past the sales counter to grab another food tray.

Wren shot me a look. "Five minutes ago you said you didn't want to help Mom with cooking in the kitchen, either. If you can't even—" Her voice caught as something grabbed her attention behind me. "Oh no. Mr. and Mrs. Lester are here."

I turned to see a ruddy-complexioned elderly man and rosy-faced woman easing themselves into a booth.

"So?"

"He's the biggest grouch on the planet," Wren whispered. "He's super picky about how we make his burger." She headed for the kitchen. "I have to warn Mom so she gets it right. Can you make two plain vanilla shakes for me? Bring them out to him right away."

"Fine." I heaved a sigh and stepped over to the shake machine as she disappeared into the kitchen.

"Plain vanilla," I muttered. *"Again."* I'd only made a dozen of these humdrum shakes in the last hour. I rolled my eyes, and my gaze fell on the rack of candy bars and gum that sat beside the self-service coffee machine.

Suddenly, inspiration struck, and I smiled. I'd surprise the socks off this stuffy Mr. Lester. That's what I'd do. I'd show him what a real shake was.

Chapter Four

I grabbed a Snickers, a Sugar Daddy, and a bag of M&M's from the candy rack and set to work. I dumped the M&M's into the large metal tumbler atop six scoops of vanilla ice cream and a hefty splash of milk. I stuck the tumbler under the silver agitator, letting the contraption blend the ingredients together into a thick, smooth, and rainbow-colored base. I poured the shake into two shake glasses and, for the "cherry on top," skewered the Snickers and Sugar Daddy onto straws. Then, with a sense that I was doing Iowa a favor with this little taste of Chicago, I whisked the shakes to the Lesters' table.

I smiled as I set the shakes down in front of them, and then stood back waiting for the compliments I was sure would come. I expected "Oohs" and "Aaahs," or a "How delightful!" Instead, Mrs. Lester brought her hands to her chest, as if she were feeling faint. Mr. Lester scowled.

"This is *not* what we ordered," he growled.

"No. It's better." My smile didn't waver. "I thought you'd like to try something new."

He scrutinized the shake from all angles, his scowl deepening. "What are all of those colors?"

"M&M's," I said proudly.

He narrowed his eyes at me. "I hate M&M's." He waved his hand at the shake. "I don't want it."

My smile tightened and my face heated. This was not how I'd imagined this going. Not at all. "Don't you want to at least try it? You might like it."

He tapped his weathered palms on the tabletop. "Young lady, I have lived a very long time. I am *done* trying new things. I know what I like, and I want what I like." He peered around me toward the kitchen. "Where is Beth? Does she know about this . . . this sugar monstrosity of yours?" he blustered, his cheeks reddening. "You're new here, and I'm going to make an official complaint—"

"That won't be necessary, Mr. Lester." Suddenly, Wren was there, steering me away from the table while smiling widely at Mr. Lester. "I'm so sorry for the confusion. We'll get you a fresh shake right away. On the house." Then she whispered to me, "*Plain*, Bria, okay? And then just try to get the rest of the orders to the right people. Go."

Cheeks burning, I stomped back to the shake machine to make one more order of vanilla shakes (grrrrrr). As I spun around with the shakes on a tray, I suddenly slammed into a teenage girl, dumping the entirety of both shakes right down her front.

"Oh my god!" she shrieked. "Look what you did!" She stared down at the milkshake avalanche oozing down her Camp Faraday T-shirt. "I have an hour bus ride back to camp, and now I have to sit in this!"

Every ounce of frustration that had been building in me over the last few hours spilled over as I stared into her fuming face. "Well, maybe you should watch where you're going!"

"Bria!" Aunt Beth's voice sounded firmly in my ear. "Take a five-minute break. I'll meet you in the kitchen."

One look at her grave face was all it took for me to know I had no choice. As she offered apologies and a free creamery T-shirt to the shake-sodden girl, I stomped toward the kitchen.

A minute later, Aunt Beth blew through the swinging doors. "That was a doozy of a spill," she said.

"Thanks to her klutziness," I snapped.

"Bria, we are in a customer service business, and—"

"I know what you're going to say. The customer's always right. Yada yada yada." I shifted from one blistered foot to the other, wincing in pain. "I don't care! All they do is complain! The food's either too cold or too hot. It takes me too long to bring it. They wanted mustard and not ketchup. They're *never* happy!"

Aunt Beth put her hand on her hip. "We're here to serve people the food they want. I thought you'd enjoy working with the customers. You didn't want to help in the kitchen."

"I don't." I dropped my serving tray on the counter with a loud clatter. "I don't want to do any of it."

Aunt Beth's lips thinned, and I dropped my eyes, feeling a stab of guilt. I loved my aunt, and part of me couldn't believe I'd just said that.

"Oh, honey, that's not really you talking."

"Who else would it be?" I blurted.

Aunt Beth only shook her head, clucking her tongue. "Now that that's out of your system, maybe we can move past it—"

Wren stuck her head around the kitchen doorway. She furrowed her eyebrows at me, and I wondered how much she'd overheard from the other side of the door. "Mom," she said. "The Vulture and his CheeseCo minions are here."

Aunt Beth gasped, pressing a hand to her forehead. "I completely forgot they were coming for the tour." Her strict demeanor faded as she sagged against a counter. "I'll be right out." She turned back to me. "Bria, go find Luke. He'll be out giving hayrides. Tell him to shut down the rides for the next hour. He'll take your spot in the dining room. Come right back to get started with your new job."

"What?" I blinked, not understanding.

Impatient, she said, "You don't want to wait tables, fine. But we all pull our weight around here. You can clean the restroom and empty the dining room trash cans."

She swept out of the kitchen without another word. Wren gave me one last glance. "Thanks for giving Mom one more thing to worry about." Then she was gone, too.

I stared after her. Was this because of CheeseCo? Why would that be my problem?

I grabbed the nearest thing I could find, a hand towel, and launched it across the room. I didn't care what punishment Aunt Beth and Uncle Troy instituted, or what punishment my parents issued long-distance from California. I was *not* cleaning restrooms.

God, what I would've given for my cell phone. I could've texted Leila and told her the thousands of ways I was hating my summer so far. Meanwhile, she was probably out shopping with friends, or having shakes at *our* special hangout (and they wouldn't just be vanilla).

Barreling out of the creamery, I nearly had another collision, this time with a group of men in suits in the parking lot. I saw the CheeseCo logo on their clipboards, and they were deep in conversation with Aunt Beth and Uncle Troy. The man talking to Aunt Beth had hunched shoulders, a face the shade of a blanched radish, and a shiny balding head that really *did* make him look like a vulture. He had to be Mr. Brannigen. I nearly laughed despite my foul mood.

I heard him say, "It's amazing your farm has survived as long as it has. Given its dilapidated state, you'd be doing yourselves a huge favor selling it. It's only a matter of time before a customer gets hurt on a hayride or rusty tractor, and then you'd have a nasty lawsuit on your hands that you can't afford." He sniffed, and gave the property a quick sweeping glance. "No need to tour the creamery," he announced as everyone else took frantic notes. "This whole building will have to go. Better to expand the milking operation."

Aunt Beth's strained expression deflated. "The creamery has a charm all its own," she started, but when Uncle Troy slid his arm around her, she stopped, as if she realized it was pointless to try to persuade Mr. Brannigen of anything.

"Why don't we start with a look at the milking barns, then?" Uncle Troy said. "You'll find our equipment is all up to code . . ."

I walked past the group and went in search of Luke, thinking I'd have to walk all the way out to the fields to find him. Instead, I was surprised when I saw him motioning to me from inside the equipment barn.

"You're supposed to go help Wren in the creamery," I said as soon as I reached him. "Nobody likes the way I deliver burger baskets."

Luke wasn't listening to a word I was saying. He was staring at his mom and dad and the CheeseCo people.

"I wish they'd just leave," he muttered. "The way Mr. Brannigen talks, you'd think CheeseCo is saving farms everywhere. Really, he's just buying up people's land at bargain prices, and kicking them out of their homes."

"I don't know. Selling the farm doesn't seem like such a bad idea to me. Your mom and dad could find better jobs."

Luke stared at me, his usual sense of humor gone. "There's *not* a better job than farming. Not for us." He settled his Dawson's Creamery cap more firmly on his head, as if to secure the farm's permanent place in the world, and started for the creamery.

As I watched him go, I caught sight of his cell phone peeking out of his back pocket. Suddenly, I was running after him, calling, "Luke, wait! Could I borrow your cell phone?" My hopes soared. "Just for a few minutes?"

He shrugged. "Sure." He pulled his phone from his pocket and tossed it to me. "Reception's terrible. You'll have to walk around until you can get a good signal."

"Thanks!" I said jubilantly, grasping the phone like the lifeline it was.

I raised it slightly over my head, staring at the screen, waiting for a few bars to appear. None did. I sidestepped the goat pen, walking first toward the milking barn and then toward the silo, without any luck. Soon, I'd made a full circle around the outbuildings without so much as a single bar of reception. I stopped in front of the gate to one of the pastures, letting out a huff of frustration. Not ready to give up, I lifted the latch and stepped into the field. There were several cows grazing a few feet away, but they didn't even glance up at me. Keeping my eyes trained on the phone, I saw one bar flicker to life. *At last!* Careful not to move the phone from its position in the air, I texted Leila.

SOS, I typed. *IT'S BRIA. ALREADY DYING OF BOREDOM. SAVE ME.*

I had just hit SEND when a chorus of *Moo*s sounded to my right. I glanced up in time to see three of the cows trotting past me, making a beeline for the open pasture gate.

I gulped, my pulse ratcheting up.

Open! The gate! I'd forgotten to latch it behind me when I'd walked through. And—oh no!—at least ten other cows had already escaped into the creamery parking lot!

I broke into a run, waving my arms at the last cows still heading for the gate, hoping I might be able to stop *any* of them.

"Hey!" I shouted. "Get back here!" I whistled, trying to keep my balance on the slippery, muddy ground.

"Come here, girls! Come on! That's a good cow!"

The cows did not come. The cows ran faster.

My voice sharpened desperately. "No! Stop!"

Suddenly, Gabe was there, stepping between me and the cows. "Don't shout." His voice was quiet and firm, his steel-gray eyes piercing. "Unless you want a stampede." For the first time since I'd met him, his patient smile was gone. He focused his attention back on the cows, now ignoring me entirely.

I blushed indignantly and tried to keep pace with him as he stepped in long, purposeful strides toward the gate.

I straightened my shoulders. "But I'm only trying to hel—" I didn't manage to finish before my feet slipped out from under me and I became airborne. With a repugnant *squelch!* I landed face-first in a giant mud puddle.

"Ew!" I shrieked, sputtering as I tried to keep the mud from splashing into my mouth and eyes. "Ew ew ew!"

I wiped at my eyes with the back of my hand, expecting that at any moment Gabe or Wren or *someone* would come to help me. I could hear excited voices and the lowing of innumerable cows. But no one came for me. Finally, I dragged myself out of the mud and glanced toward the parking lot, where Luke, Wren, Gabe, Aunt Beth, and Uncle Troy were all busy herding the cows away from customers and the CheeseCo entourage and back toward the pasture.

"This is exactly the sort of situation that would never happen under CheeseCo management," Mr. Brannigen was saying, and then he stepped in a pile of cow manure, and the rest of his words were lost in an indecipherable rant as, red faced and scowling, he made for his car.

Aunt Beth called an apology after him, while Wren and Luke didn't even try to hide their grins.

Out of everyone, it was Gabe who had the most command of the situation, talking to the cows in a low, quiet voice that calmed them. He was coaxing the cows slowly back into the field, and like children under the magic spell of a pied piper, they serenely followed him.

I picked my way over to my aunt and cousins, wringing muddy water from my shirt and hair as I went. "I'm so sorry," I blustered, handing Luke back his miraculously clean phone. "I was only trying to send a text message, and I went into the pasture to get better reception. I guess I forgot to latch the gate."

"It's all right," Aunt Beth said distractedly, and then quickly turned back to the remaining customers, offering free milkshakes to everyone. Wren, Luke, and Uncle Troy were just as busy reassuring customers, too.

"I'm sorry," I said again helplessly, but no one seemed to hear except Gabe. Even though there was a look of dismay on his face, he laughed softly. "I've got to hand it to you, Bria." He shook his head. "You're having a killer first day."

Heated embarrassment flashed over me as he secured the gate behind the last cow. "Why is there a Wi-Fi hot spot in the middle of a stinking field anyway?"

He grinned again, making me want to smack him. "Look. You don't know what you're doing." He said it gently, but it still stung. "Just stay out of the pasture so my cows don't get hurt."

"The *cows*?" I blurted. "*Your* cows? What about *me*?"

He brushed past me, his broad shoulders shaking with laughter, and disappeared into the milking barn. I stared after him, fuming.

"You okay?" Wren appeared at my elbow, looking me up and down. "I don't see any hoof prints on you. Just mud."

"I hate mud," I grumbled, but my eyes were still fixed on the door of the milking barn.

Wren retrieved a boot that I hadn't even realized I'd lost from the mud puddle nearby.

"I can't believe Gabe's Mr. High and Mighty act," I said stiffly. "He didn't even care that I almost got trampled!"

Wren poured a dollop of mud out of my shoe and handed it back to me. She did *not* look happy. "Our cows wouldn't know how to stampede if they were being chased by a pack of wolves."

I huffed. "He didn't have to be rude. He knows I'm new."

A second later, Luke was beside us, grinning. "Well, cuz, I've been wanting Mr. Brannigen to step in it for a while now, and I just want to say . . . thank you." He bowed jokingly. "Because today you granted my wish."

He laughed, but I wasn't in the mood. "I'm going to get cleaned up," I said, and with that, marched to the house, leaving a trail of muddy footprints behind me.

Killer first day indeed.

Chapter Five

You don't know what you're doing. Gabe's teasing words ran a repeating loop through my head, and my blood boiled as I sat at the dinner table, picking at the fried pork tenderloin. I could barely even look his way.

"Bria." Aunt Beth jolted me from my thoughts. "You've barely touched your food."

"Just not very hungry," I mumbled.

"I'm starving!" Luke boasted around a mouthful of mashed potatoes. "Must've been chasing after the runaway cows that did it." He snorted a laugh into his napkin as Wren slapped him on the arm.

"C'mon, Luke." Gabe elbowed him in the ribs, and then shot me a sympathetic look, which I pointedly ignored. Did he actually think being nice to me now could make up for humiliating me earlier?

But Uncle Troy chuckled, too. "That was one to remember, all right. The Great Cow Escape. Oh, our customers' faces . . . they didn't know whether to laugh or run for their lives." He and Luke howled even harder then, until Uncle Troy was wiping at his eyes with the back of his hand.

"Boys." Aunt Beth included Uncle Troy in her scolding stare. "Enough. Let poor Bria eat her dinner in peace, will you?"

"Actually, I'm finished anyway." I stood up to bring my dish to the sink. "Is it okay if I watch *Gossip High* on the TV? It's on Netflix."

"Sorry, sweetie," Aunt Beth said. "We don't have Netflix."

"Wha—oh!" I must've looked miserable, because Gabe stood up then, too.

"The weather's perfect for night fishing," he said.

"I'm in." Luke was already jumping up from the table.

"Is there ever a time when you *don't* want to go night fishing?" Aunt Beth laughed and tried to ruffle Luke's hair but he immediately ducked out from under her hand.

Gabe turned toward me. "Have you ever been night fishing?" he asked.

"No," I answered. "I love eating fish. *Not* the idea of catching them. And at night?" Visions of mosquitoes and wriggly, slimy worms squirmed before my eyes.

"You wouldn't like it," Wren said to me. "Too dirty." There was a certain satisfaction in her tone that irritated me, as if she was banking on my failure, yet again.

"She can decide that for herself," Gabe said. "You don't seem like the giving-up sort," he told me. "But then again . . ." He winked. "Maybe dirt already got the better of you."

"It *didn't*." I set my teeth. Now that he was turning this into a dare, how could I possibly say no? I met his eyes dead-on, unflinching. "I'm in."

He smiled, like he'd just won a small victory. "See you outside in ten."

The moment he was gone through the door, I sank back against the kitchen wall. I wanted to prove Gabe wrong, but . . . night fishing? I cringed. What had I just gotten myself into?

"How much farther?" I picked my way precariously through the knee-high grass, my eyes trained on the flashlight beam.

Nobody responded, and I had the distinct impression that, even though I'd been invited along, I wasn't necessarily welcome.

Wren and Luke walked ahead of me, talking in hushed, worried tones. I'd picked up the word *CheeseCo* more than once, so I guessed they were rehashing their parents' meeting with the dairy company. I didn't understand why it should be upsetting them so much, but Wren, especially, seemed out of sorts over it, her voice rising into pinched pitches here and there.

Gabe was walking at a steady pace, his head down, tackle box and fishing rod in hand. Since I didn't want to be walking alone, I was hustling to keep pace with him. The tepid summer night air was filled with strange sounds: clicks and hums and chirps, the rustling of the tall grass, and the lowing of the cows. Mosquitoes buzzed about, until I was swatting at them almost constantly, even though I'd sprayed enough bug repellent on me to ward off Iowa's entire insect population.

"Ugh, these bugs," I said. "They're everywhere."

"That's bugs for you." Gabe's matter-of-fact tone made irritation burble inside me fresh. Why was he always so calm, so unaffected?

Suddenly, something large swooped through the darkness over my head, flapping its wings furiously. I shrieked and ducked, and a second later felt a warm arm around my shoulders.

"Only a bat." Gabe's voice came soft beside my ear, and might have been comforting if there hadn't been the lightness of laughter around its edges.

I shrugged off his arm and stood, brushing invisible dirt from my capris. "A bat? God, what if it bit me? Or scratched me? Don't they carry rabies?"

"It didn't get near you. It was just eating those bugs you hate so much."

"Why am I even out here?" I blurted. I glanced toward the

distant lights of the house. The idea of going back was tempting. *So tempting.*

"You're out here," Gabe said then, "because some people might think you can't handle it. And you don't want to prove them right."

I stopped walking to stare at him. "Are you one of those people? Who think I don't belong here?"

He turned to face me. "I'm the only biracial kid in my entire school. Pretty much this whole county." He shrugged. "I don't make a big deal out of it, but I'll never tell anybody they don't belong."

I nodded. Gabe wouldn't stand out in my school in Chicago, where my classmates came from all kinds of backgrounds. But in this tiny town, it sounded like he did. "But . . . you still like living here?"

"Sure I do. My friends are *kinda* cool." He laughed and jerked his head jokingly toward Luke. "And our school has an awesome agricultural program. I'll get to enroll next year. Plus, I don't think I could live anywhere that didn't have open spaces. I wouldn't be able to breathe in a big city—"

He stopped and pointed toward the cornfield.

"Look there," he whispered. "It's an owl hunting. See it?"

At first I didn't, but then a fluttering movement caught my eye, and there it was, an owl with wings spread, brushing the tops of the corn stalks.

"How do you do that?" I asked him. "It's like you have Spidey senses. You see everything."

He laughed. "I spend almost all my time outside. I just pay attention."

"Hey!" Wren's voice called from the darkness up ahead. "You guys coming or what?"

We doubled our pace, and a minute later, the pond came into view, along with two rowboats resting side by side along its shore. A million silver crescents rippled across the pond's surface, and I supposed, for a moment, that it was pretty.

"Best largemouth bass around." Luke beamed proudly, wasting no time plunking his tackle box and pole into one of the boats.

To me and Gabe, Wren said, "Luke will take you—"

"Bria can come with me," Gabe interrupted as he placed his gear into the second boat. He motioned for me to have a seat.

Wren hesitated for a split second, seeming almost as confused as I was by Gabe's announcement. But I joined him as he slid the boat smoothly into the water and quickly climbed in. The boat rocked unsteadily as he took his seat, and I clutched the side of it.

"Don't lean to one side like that," Gabe advised as he took up the oars. "You'll make the boat tilt. And keep your voice down or you'll scare the fish." I quickly moved to the center of my bench, and he cocked his head at me, adding, "You've never been on a boat before."

"I've been on boats," I whisper-hissed. "I've taken water taxis around Chicago and the Lake Express ferry once, but . . ." Confession time. ". . . I've never been in a rowboat."

"Nothing to it," Gabe said confidently.

"Are there life jackets?" I asked uncertainly, peering under my bench.

He laughed and leaned toward me, his eyes glinting. "The pond's not that deep, Bria. You can swim, right?"

"I better not have to swim," I countered. Wren and Luke's boat wasn't too far yet, and I caught Wren's eye as she watched us curiously. She looked quickly away. Yup, she was annoyed with me.

Around the pond, every tree and shrub, the fences that ran alongside the pastures, the corn and bean fields—all of it had morphed into ghostly black shadows.

"I can't get over how dark it is," I said. "In Chicago, there are lights twenty-four seven. The city's so bright you can't ever see stars."

"No stars," Gabe said. "Sounds awful."

"It's actually beautiful," I said, thinking of home. "Like there are stars inside the skyscrapers. And there kind of are, if you think about it. Dozens of families sitting down to dinner in an apartment building, hundreds of people working inside an office building, thousands of people living all in one square city block."

I'd forgotten for a second who I was talking to, and I glanced at Gabe now, my cheeks heating with embarrassment. He'd paused in rowing and was staring at me, an indiscernible expression on his face. Then he blinked, cleared his throat, and took up rowing again.

"All man-made." I could hear his distaste in his voice. "The skyscrapers, the lights. Not an ounce of nature to any of it."

"That doesn't mean it's not beautiful," I said defensively.

He looked at the sky over our heads. "To me, that's beautiful." I followed his gaze, and for the first time, saw what I hadn't before. Lacy spirals of stars splashed across the sky. I'd never seen so many stars all at once, and shining so brightly.

"It is," I admitted softly. "Too bad you have to be in the boring boondocks to see it."

I felt, more than saw, him stiffen at that.

Beside us came a sudden splash, and I jumped.

"Just the fish biting," Gabe said, seeming happy to change the subject. He tucked the oars into the boat and surveyed the pond's surface. "This is a good spot for casting." He nodded to the pole at my feet, and a lidded Styrofoam cup of bait. "I'll bait the hook for you." He reached for the pole, already running on the assumption that I was clueless.

"No, I've got it," I said quickly, overcome with the urge to prove that I didn't need his help. My parents had taken me fishing at the Riverwalk once when I was eight, but I hadn't caught anything. Still, I *did* remember how to bait a hook (or, I thought I remembered, at least).

I grabbed the bait cup and pried off the lid. I peered inside, expecting to find the usual dirt and pink, wriggling worms. Instead, I found a mass of sluggish black . . .

"Leeches!" I screamed, and, without thinking, leapt up, dumping the cup's contents into my lap. Leeches spilled onto my pants and shirt, and I screamed again. "Get them off, get them off!" I hopped from one foot to the other, swiping at the leeches all over me, as the boat swayed precariously.

Faintly, I heard Wren and Luke calling to me from their boat, urging me to calm down, but I was too far gone for reason.

"Bria, sit down," Gabe warned, holding up his hands. "The boat's going to—"

The boat didn't tip, but I did. Right over the side of the boat and into the water, belly flopping with a resounding *splash*! Even though it was summer, the water was startlingly cold, and I came up spluttering and breathless, wiping water and pond grass from my eyes.

"Are you okay?" Wren's voice came through the darkness, but

with it came Luke's stifled giggles, followed by the sound of a smack on the arm that cut him off.

I was surprised, with as much heated anger as I felt in that moment, that the water around me wasn't boiling.

Gabe was leaning over the side of the boat, his hand extended toward me. "Give me your hand." Even in the dim light, I could see the glint of merriment on his face. He thought this was funny!

"No. Way." I clenched my teeth as I treaded water. "You did that on purpose! You could've warned me, at least! Who uses leeches for bait? Who does that?"

He laughed. "Bria, you said you wanted to bait the hook—"

"I didn't know!" I whirled in the water and swam as fast as I could toward shore. With adrenaline and anger fueling me, it only took a minute before I was straggling from the pond, dripping wet and shivering. Gabe was seconds behind me in the boat.

He'd been rowing beside me the entire time, I realized, but I'd been too furious to notice.

I glared at him. "How could you do that to me?" I seethed. "As if today hasn't been bad enough, you have to make me feel like a total idiot, too?"

"Bria," he said softly. "Come on. Nobody saw except us and the fish. And, you have to admit, it's pretty funny."

"Funny?!" I jabbed a finger into his chest. "I'm not here for your entertainment. I'm not some . . . some joke!"

I stared into his eyes, waiting for him to yell back. Waiting for him to tell me how stuck-up and spoiled I was, how ludicrous with my city-girl shrieking and desperate pasture-texting.

Instead, he just stood there, holding out a towel toward me.

His refusal to engage was even more aggravating than anything he could've said.

"Bria." Wren was climbing out of the other boat, hurrying over, but I was done. I was done with all of them.

"I'm going." I snatched the towel from Gabe's hand. "And no, I don't need help. I can find my way back just fine."

Chapter Six

I flipped over in bed for the hundredth time and curled the pillow around my ears to try to mute the deafening hum of crickets. It didn't work. Even though I'd taken a very long bath and freed myself of all green pond scum and made sure no leeches had followed me indoors, I couldn't stop imagining the look on Gabe's face, the unchecked amusement in his eyes.

I sat up and threw off the covers, then tiptoed past Wren's sleeping form and downstairs to the family room. The computer was still on, displaying its screensaver photo montage of family pictures.

I sat down just as a photo of me slid by. I was around five, and the very same pond I'd floundered in tonight was behind me, sparkling in the sun. I was holding up my splayed, mud-covered hands to the camera, grinning happily, splattered head to toe in mud.

I didn't remember posing for that photo, or there ever being a time when I was *that* muddy. I'd liked it, too! An inexplicable sadness swept over me, and for a fleeting second, I almost wished I could go back to the version of me in that photo. As quickly as it had come, I shook the thought away. No. I didn't *want* to go back to that. I was a new me now, a better me.

I clicked the mouse, hoping beyond hope that the internet would actually be working, despite the finicky Wi-Fi. I let out a breath as the search engine flickered to life.

I pulled up my email, watching anxiously as my inbox loaded. There'd be something from Leila, I was sure. But, instead of an email from Leila, there was one from—shocker—Jane. I winced at the sight of her name, unsure whether I should open it or not. Maybe it would be the confrontation I'd been waiting for, the "I know what you did" note that blamed me for everything. But when I opened it, the email read:

Hey Bria,

I know we haven't talked much lately, but your mom called my mom and asked if I would send you a note. I'm not sure why. She said something about you being away for the summer and how you'd like to hear from me. I don't think that's true, but you know how my mom gets about stuff like this. She logs into my email every once in a while to make sure I'm using it "appropriately," blah blah blah. If she sees I didn't email you, I'll get the whole lecture about friendship and responsibility . . .

I laughed when I read that, knowing how true it was. I kept reading.

Anyway . . . hi. Hope you're having a nice summer.

Jane

My heart squeezed tight as I reread the email. I thought I'd be relieved that she hadn't written "I miss you," or "Why don't we hang out anymore?" but the clamminess in my chest didn't feel like relief. It felt like regret.

I shut down the computer. I didn't want to think about the fact that Jane had emailed me, or the fact that Leila hadn't.

I wanted . . . I wanted . . . My spirits lifted a smidge. All I wanted was a Sip & Shake milkshake—a taste of the city I missed. Shakes weren't as complicated as friendships. They didn't need apologies or emails to work. Plus, the one I'd made Mr. Lester had looked so good, and I hadn't gotten a chance to taste it.

I made my way to the kitchen, checking the wall clock. It was close to midnight. Using the blender would be loud and might wake everyone up. But I could shut the doors to the kitchen to keep the noise down. It would be quiet enough.

Peeking into the freezer, my heart bolstered at the sight of gallons of Dawson's Creamery Homemade Ice Cream. There were only the tried-and-true predictable flavors, of course: vanilla, chocolate, and strawberry. But a quick search through the kitchen pantry revealed a stash of mini candy bars, a bag of marshmallows, a box of graham crackers, and bars of chocolate. Even better, there were some fresh-baked chocolate chip cookies left over from dinner.

I lined up all the ingredients for a gourmet shake on the counter beside the blender. My shake for Mr. Lester had just been a warm-up; I knew I could accessorize even better now, just how I always did with my fave outfits. Wasn't I always telling Leila that the simplest pair of pants could be fabulous with a sparkly belt or eye-popping shoes? All I needed to make a shake as glamouriffic as the ones at Sip & Shake was a little flair here and there.

Starting with the base, I scooped four big scoops of vanilla ice cream into the blender, then splashed in some milk. I surveyed the array of candy bars, cookies, and chocolate before me, and decided on tossing in four mini Heath bars and two Twix. Then, making sure the kitchen doors were shut, I turned on the blender. It revved to life and the mixture swirled before my eyes, checkered with bits of Heath and Twix. Already, it looked delicious. I stopped the blender and poured the thick shake into a mason jar, taste testing with my finger as I poured. YUM. It was almost there, but not quite.

I stuck three straws into the shake. I skewered one whole Twix bar onto one straw and three marshmallows onto the other. Still, it needed the finishing touch. I squirted a hefty mountain of Reddi-wip on top of the milkshake, then set one of Aunt Beth's chocolate chip cookies on top. I smiled. Perfection.

I sat down at the kitchen table with the shake and took a long, much-needed sip. It tasted even better than it looked, the Heath and Twix mixing into a nutty, caramel flavor that was satisfying and sweet. I was about to dip the cookie into the shake when, suddenly, the door to the kitchen swung open, and Wren's sleepy-eyed, pillow-creased face appeared.

"What are you *doing*?" She rubbed her eyes grumpily, then stared at the candy wrappers and drips of ice cream and milk strewn across the kitchen counter. "Are you crazy? What is *that*?" She jabbed an accusatory finger at my shake.

"It's . . ." I sat back, trying to think of a fittingly outlandish name for my shake, like the ones back home. "It's a Twixie Tornado."

She sank into one of the chairs. "Didn't the shake you made for Mr. Lester teach you anything?" she asked, studying my shake. But she didn't look put off by it. In fact, now that her eyes were open all the way, she looked kind of . . . hungry.

"Nobody actually tasted my shake this afternoon. This is how we do them in Chicago," I said. "A little less boring."

She raised her eyebrow at me. "Do you think you could drop your attitude for five seconds?"

"I don't know," I countered. "Could you drop yours?"

"Mine?" Her tone was incredulous. "I'm not the one who's above working. You stuck me with bathroom cleanup today, plus everything else." She locked eyes with me. "It's not fair, what you're doing. It's only stressing Mom and Dad out, and they don't need any more stress."

"Right, 'cause milking cows is really stressful." As soon as the words left my mouth, an arrow of guilt pierced my heart. Wren's head jerked back as if she'd been slapped. "I'm sorry," I blurted. "I didn't mean—"

"You have no idea what you're talking about," she snapped. "You think what we do is just for fun?" She glared at me until I couldn't take it and hung my head.

"No," I said quietly. "I don't think that. I saw how hard you worked today. I don't know what made me say that. I really am sorry."

"You don't know a thing about our lives, or what we're going through right now." Her angry tone sank into sadness, and she suddenly looked so glum, I had to at least *try* to ask her about it.

"Do you mean the CheeseCo thing?"

She sighed. "If they buy our farm, we'll have to move."

"To someplace else in Tillman?"

She shook her head. "Mom says she'd want us to live closer to you guys."

"To us?" My voice betrayed my disbelief. "But you don't even like visiting us in the city!"

"Tell me about it," she mumbled. "It would suck beyond imagining. I don't ever want to leave the farm. I love it." She looked up at me. "I want to run it someday."

I opened my mouth, about to tell her she couldn't possibly know what she wanted to do when she was grown-up already. But the unwavering determination in her eyes stopped me. She meant every word of what she'd just said.

Both of us sat in silence as my shake began to melt and the cookie on top started to get soggy. Some of the anger I'd felt all day was leaking out of me, and I thought from Wren's sagging shoulders that hers was, too. With a sigh, I pushed the shake closer to her and handed her a spoon. "Want to try some?"

She weighed her options for a second, and I imagined her trying to decide whether or not we'd both survive the summer if we kept up like this. Ultimately, she accepted my peace offering and took a tentative bite.

"It's good."

I laughed. "You don't have to sound so shocked."

"Ha!" Her short laugh came then, and she took a second bite as I leaned in to sip some of the shake through the straw. The coolness of it seemed to work some kind of magic, extinguishing the last remnants of our irritation.

"Why did you even come here if you hate it so much?" Wren asked.

"I didn't have a choice." I slumped back against my chair. "Mom and Dad made me come."

"What do you mean?"

"Like as punishment." I fidgeted with the straw in the shake. "I'm friends with someone they don't like. I think they hope that being here will change my mind about her."

Wren broke off a piece of the cookie and dunked it into the shake. "Why don't they like her?"

I swallowed, unease sweeping over me. I wasn't sure I wanted to talk about this. Even thinking about it made a cold fish of nervousness flip-flop in my stomach. On the other hand, it would be nice—comforting even—if Wren saw things from my point of view. Just for a moment.

"Leila got into trouble a couple of months ago," I said slowly. "She got an in-school suspension. She has her own YouTube channel; she posts critiques of people's clothes at our school. She took pics of some kids' outfits to use in her video. She didn't post faces or names, but everybody knew who they were anyway."

Wren snorted. "I bet she would've had a blast with my wardrobe."

"Oh, she would've," I said before I could stop myself. I glanced at her guiltily. "Sorry."

She shrugged. "I know I'm fashion-challenged. I couldn't care less." But there was the tiniest hitch in her voice that made me wonder if that was really true. "So then what happened?"

My pulse quickened. "I wasn't in the video and I didn't film it. But . . ." I rubbed my damp hands on my pajama pants. "I helped Leila come up with the outfits she talked about. I didn't know she was going to use them in a video. We were just hanging out one day after school and she said, 'Hey, what are some of the worst outfits you've seen so far this year?'"

"So you gave her some ideas," Wren said.

I nodded, deciding not to tell Wren the part about how I included my former best friend's outfits in the list we made. That *I* was the one who'd pointed out Jane's latest tacky, colorful getup that had made it into the video. Even now, I didn't like to think about it.

"Anyway," I said, "Leila told her parents that I'd been involved, and they told *my* parents and . . ." I shrugged. "Bottom line is that they don't want me spending time with her."

"I can't believe she ratted you out to her parents," Wren said, "or that she'd post something like that in the first place. Seems really mean to me."

"But she's not," I insisted. "She's . . . she's the sort of person who makes everything look so effortless. And she's so confident."

"How confident can she be if she's making fun of other people?"

I frowned. "She did something stupid. But she's not a bad person. She's always letting me put together outfits for her, and she says I have an amazing fashion sense."

"Letting you?" Wren raised an eyebrow. "What are you, her personal dresser?"

"It's not like that." I bristled. "I've always loved mixing and matching outfits. I do it for her because I want to."

"Those earrings you had on today were cool," Wren admitted. "Not that I could ever pull them off, but—"

"You totally could!" I said excitedly. "Omigod, you could wear them with this purple maxi dress I have, and—"

"Uh-uh." Wren shook her head. "Save your extreme makeovers for Leila. As long as she's not just using you." I squirmed uncomfortably, and Wren picked up on it. "I mean, I don't know her. She's not my friend. She's yours."

I nodded, relieved that I wasn't going to get yet another lecture from someone about choosing friends wisely. I'd heard enough of that from Mom and Dad lately.

"Is it really so awful," Wren asked quietly, "being here?"

"It's not me," I said simply.

She shook her head. "You're so different now."

"You say it like it's a bad thing," I said, feeling some of my defensiveness return. "Why does *everyone* think that it's so terrible? What if I *want* to be different?"

"I liked who you were before," she said quietly.

When we were smaller, the fact that our lives were poles apart hadn't seemed to matter as much. We'd played on the tire swing hanging from the rafters of the livestock barn, built forts with

Legos, made messes in the kitchen baking cookies with Mom and Aunt Beth. But now Wren was as dug into her life here as I was into mine, and our mismatched personalities seemed all the more magnified.

I stared at the empty glass between us. The milkshake was gone.

Wren stood. "I'm sorry you hate it here so much, but here's the thing. Luke might not care, but I'm not going to put up with you sitting on your butt all summer doing squat." Her voice was as hard and impenetrable as a tank. If I hadn't been a little intimidated, I might've been impressed. "We can spend the summer annoyed with each other, or we can make it work. Your choice."

She walked out, leaving me in the kitchen, alone with my thoughts. I didn't have to listen to her. I mean, what was she going to do? Put leeches in my bed? I shuddered. She wouldn't . . . would she? I couldn't be absolutely sure. She was tough. But . . . she was also scared. I'd seen it on her face tonight when she talked about CheeseCo. If she had to move, Wren would be facing a world as alien to her as the farm was alien to me. My guess was that it wouldn't be any easier for her to deal with, either. Maybe I could cut her a little slack by doing what she asked.

I stood to clean up my kitchen adventures. So . . . I'd suffer through the chores. It would be torture, but I didn't have to do them well. I just had to survive them.

Chapter Seven

The next few days passed as a series of small disasters. It was as if I were in one of those movies where the main character has to relive the same day over and over again, waiting to finally get it right.

I woke up to Wren's blaring alarm each morning and ignored it until I either dragged myself out of bed or Uncle Troy appeared with the ice water (I'd only been doused one time, but that was one time too many). Then, while Luke, Wren, and Gabe helped with the milking, I mucked out the goat pen, trying to ward off Tulip, the lunatic goat who'd developed an appetite for my clothing. Gabe, I'd realized, always checked the pen after me, and always mucked it out properly.

He hadn't spoken a word to me since the night fishing fiasco, but I caught him glancing my way as I went about the farm chores, even daring to make exaggerated moping faces at me. If he passed me in the farmyard, he started up a whistling rendition of "There Ain't No Bugs on Me." Luke thought it was hilarious. I didn't. If Gabe was trying to win me over with that ridiculous behavior, he had another thing coming. I was still mad at him. I'd *stay* mad.

After the outdoor chores were done, I would help Aunt Beth and Wren in the creamery. *Help*, though, was a strong word for what I did. I messed up so many food orders that customers actually started looking frightened when I approached their tables.

"Maybe it's better for you to work behind the scenes," Aunt Beth suggested diplomatically after a few too many spilled trays. "Wren says you can make a decent shake, so let's put you on shake detail."

I was secretly pleased with the new assignment, because of all the jobs I might've been given, mixing up milkshakes was definitely the easiest. But by the end of that first week, I was sick of boring milkshakes, too. Plus, I still hadn't heard from Leila, and when I talked to my parents, they went on and on about how great their time in California was. It was enough to make me want to scream in frustration.

Which is almost what I did now, as Wren tapped me on the shoulder with an order for two more vanilla milkshakes.

"You're kidding," I moaned. "I've made twenty already today. Don't these people ever want something new?"

"It's the Lesters again," Wren said. "Don't mess up this time. Please. He asked for Mom specifically, but she's out in the pasture. Matilda's gone lame and Mom and Gabe are trying to bring her into the barn so the vet can take a look." Wren took off her apron. "I need to go help."

"What?" Panic rose in my throat. "You can't leave me here by myself—"

"Bria." Wren sighed. "All you have to do is take the Lesters' order and have my dad get their burger baskets ready." She was already walking through the door. "That's it. Impossible to mess up."

But, of course, it was not impossible, as I realized when I set down the order in front of Mr. and Mrs. Lester. It only took a nanosecond for him to frown.

"This shake's watery."

I eyed the shake mug, taking in the thick swirl of vanilla at its top. "It looks fine to me. I just made it."

"Take it back," he snapped. "Your aunt can make me a new one."

My hands fisted at my sides. "My aunt's not here right now," I said through clenched teeth. "And you don't have to be so rude all the time, you know."

"*I'm* rude?" He threw his napkin down on his seat. "Wait until your aunt hears about this—"

"Tell her whatever you want," I blurted so loudly that other customers turned heads in our direction. "Go ahead! I don't care!"

I spun away and slammed straight into Gabe, who was standing there alongside Aunt Beth and Wren. They'd seen the entire outburst unfold. Shame flashed over me. I opened my mouth to defend myself, but looking into my aunt's shocked face, all words left me. I pushed past them and ran headlong out the door.

On my way past the livestock barn, I found myself stopping inside to see the old tire swing. Memories from childhood, previously fuzzy around the edges, crystallized now. I had a vision of

Mom pushing me on this swing, of me and Wren swinging together with our heads thrown back in laughter. Mom had told me once that the swing had been here since she was little. Now I climbed onto it, pushing myself off the ground with one foot. The swing swooped upward through golden beams of dust motes, and I took a long, big breath at the top. As I got back to the bottom, I saw Gabe step into the barn.

His dark curls caught the sunlight, and the way his forearms were crossed against his chest, I could see every tendon outlined under his skin. My heart leapt against my will. Why did he have to be cute when he was so completely unnerving in every possible way?

"Well, at least you get along with the tire swing," he said with that half-curling smile. "Too bad it's not one of the creamery customers."

I clambered off the swing. "Yeah, well, the swing wouldn't tell me off in front of a room full of people."

"Mr. Lester wasn't exactly telling you off, but . . ." He shrugged. "You see what you want to see, I guess."

"What's that supposed to mean?" I started toward him. "I haven't done a thing to him. I did *not* give him a watery shake today. And when I offered him something new to try, it was like his world was ending!" I dug the toe of my shoe into the hay strewn across the barn's floor. "It's just so typical. As far as everyone around here is concerned, anything outside the confines of Tillman, Iowa, doesn't matter. Or even exist."

Gabe shook his head, rubbing the back of his neck and mumbling something indecipherable.

"What?" I pushed, "You think I'm wrong?"

He began to walk away, then stopped and faced me. "I think Mr. Lester's not the only one being stubborn about the way everything should be."

I balked. "You mean *me*?"

"Do you ever listen to yourself?" His gray eyes darkened into two swirling storms, all trace of amusement gone from his face. "You criticize everyone here for not wanting to try new things. But you're doing the same thing."

"What are you talking about? Everything I've been doing around here is something new. Mucking poop and waiting tables and—"

"But you haven't been giving any of it a fair chance. Not really. I tried to show you the ropes. I wanted to help." He shook his head. "I get what it's like to feel out of place. But . . . your attitude is *your* choice." With a deep breath, he said, "Here's what I think. You've been sabotaging your jobs, hoping it will eventually get you out of them." His eyes never left my face, and for the first time, I saw real disappointment in them.

I swallowed, dropping my gaze to avoid his. "That's not true—"

"Isn't it? You take the shovel into the goat pen without scooping up a single thing. You pick fights with customers in the creamery. And you know good and well that Wren or Luke or I will clean up your mistakes."

"I—I . . ." My voice drowned in my throat.

"Do whatever you like, but know this." His face was resigned, his voice soft but immovable all at once. "I love my mom and dad, but they both work long hours. This right here's my second family.

I don't want the Dawsons to sell to CheeseCo any more than Luke and Wren do. You have no idea how much work they put into this farm, or how much it means to them. So if you're not going to help them, then stay out of my way. Because I am."

With that final resounding word, he spun on his heel and was gone, without as much as a glance back in my direction.

I wanted to call him back. I wanted to argue, to tell him how wrong he was. But—much as I hated to even contemplate the possibility—was he right about me? I hadn't intended to wreck every task I'd been given since coming here, but maybe there had been a part of me—a bigger part than I cared to admit—that had wanted, even hoped, to fail.

I saw Wren and Luke approaching. They were leading Matilda, her leg bandaged neatly by the vet, into the barn.

"Hey, guys," I started, "about what happened in the creamery—"

"Save it," Wren snapped, and Luke's silence indicated he didn't want to hear anything from me, either. I was debating whether or not I should try to explain again, when Aunt Beth called me back toward the house. I jogged over to where she was waiting.

"Park it." She pointed to one of the outside benches, her face stony. "We need to talk."

I sank onto the bench. "It wasn't my fault! I was only—"

"No more excuses." Her voice seeped disappointment, but also tiredness. I noticed the dark circles under her eyes. She sat down beside me, and moved her hand as if to take mine, but stopped. "When your mom called me to see if you could stay this summer, I was thrilled." She smiled sadly. "Baby, I've always loved you like I love Wren and Luke. And your mom's been worried about you—"

"I'm sick of hearing that," I said.

I expected her to argue or push, but she didn't. She clasped and unclasped her hands in her lap. "Here's the thing. Your uncle and I are up to our eyeballs in work. We've got the Fourth of July Bash coming up, and one of the milking machines bit the dust this morning. And we have some big decisions to make about CheeseCo, which I'm none too happy about." She rubbed her temples. "I've been giving you the benefit of the doubt, but I'm also not going to wage a war with you all summer long, either. If you don't want to do the farm chores, fine. But you still have to help around the house. No getting out of dishes or making your bed. Understood?"

I nodded, too stunned to say anything. She was actually letting me off the hook! No more goat pellets or four-forty-five wake-up calls. I could sleep in! I could veg all day.

"Thanks, Aunt Beth," I said, and I meant it. "About Mom and Dad. Are you—"

"Going to tell them about this?" Aunt Beth said, reading my mind. She nodded. "Have to, honey. Your mom and I don't keep secrets from each other." She stood. "Go on back to the house. We'll see you later this afternoon."

Then she left me alone on the bench, with a free pass to spend my afternoon however I wanted. I jumped to my feet and, with a spring in my step, hurried to the house. First I would email Leila. Then I'd check out her latest fashion video. After that? The sky was the limit.

Chapter Eight

My first afternoon of computer time and lounging around the house was *glorious*. It was maybe a little too quiet, but I could do whatever I wanted. As the hours dragged on, though, I started to get a taste of what avoiding farm life actually meant. I'd thought it was bad being included in all the chores, but over the next two days, I started to think maybe it was worse *not* being included. As everyone else went about their routines, I found it hard to look them in the eyes.

Wren didn't set her alarm; instead, Uncle Troy tiptoed in quietly to wake her. I thought I'd be able to enjoy sleeping in, but I still awoke when I heard the muffled sounds of breakfast drifting up from the kitchen. And without any chores besides occasional dishes and laundry, my days in the empty house felt long.

I avoided the creamery and the barns. I kept mostly to myself, barely talking to the others during dinner and afterward, reading until bedtime. When I half joked to Mom and Dad over the phone about how much summer reading I could get done now that I wasn't doing farm chores, they didn't laugh. I couldn't stop thinking about how I was letting everyone down.

Only Leila, in the first email she sent, offered me any consolation. *Good for you for standing up to tyranny*, she'd written. *Serves your family right for trying to put you to work. Nobody should have to spend their summer shoveling manure.*

I tried to take comfort in her words, but I just couldn't. She was making my family out to sound like some kind of cruel dictatorship, and that didn't sit right with me. Still, I wrote her back a thank-you, and told her how much I missed her.

On the third morning, after *finally* sleeping in until eleven (hallelujah!), I was grabbing a bagel from the kitchen, feeling the full weight of the house's silence around me, when I peered out the kitchen window. I saw a stream of summer camp buses pouring into the creamery parking lot, and kids tumbling out of the buses by the dozens. There were way more kids than there were seats in the creamery, and I imagined the chaos of all of them vying to order as Wren and Aunt Beth scrambled to cook and ring up the orders.

Surprising myself, I headed for the front door. I couldn't stay in this too-still house a second longer. And besides, there was no way Aunt Beth and Wren could handle that crowd.

Doesn't matter, Leila's voice whispered in my head. *Not your problem.*

But I didn't have to work at the creamery all day. I'd only stay until the crowd thinned.

When I stepped into the little restaurant, the voices of a hundred excited camp kids crashed over me in a deafening wave. Kids were climbing over the backs of the booths, wrestling in line, and blowing spit wads at one another through straws. It was madness.

I waded through the crowd to the sales counter, where Wren was frantically taking orders. She frowned at me.

"What are you doing here?" she asked as she pushed buttons on the cash register.

My cheeks burned, but I decided to ignore her harsh tone. I said simply, "You need help."

She raised a skeptical eyebrow. "I thought you were above helping."

Ouch. That one stung. "I . . ." I swallowed. "I deserved that."

She did a double take, and I nearly laughed. Surprise wasn't a look I saw very often on Wren's face.

I drew in a breath. "Look, I want a second chance, because . . . I'm sorry. About the way I've been acting. I might've messed up a few things on purpose, but I want to try for real."

I could see she didn't want to give me another chance, but there were also half a dozen customers already complaining about the service taking too long. She didn't have a choice.

"Fine." She slapped an apron into my hand. "You're sorry? Prove it."

I nodded. "Where should I start?"

"I need six *plain* vanilla shakes. ASAP."

"On it," I said, but she was already consumed in ringing up the next order. I made the shakes quickly and, even though it pained me to do it, exactly like Wren had told me to—plain. Then, I brought the order to the customers' table, without spilling a single drop.

When I returned to the sales counter, I discovered a teen in a camp counselor uniform giving Wren a hard time about the shake menu.

"I can't believe you only have three flavors," she was saying, her voice dripping with dissatisfaction. "We drove two hours from camp for *this*? You don't even have anything *close* to a Snickerdoodle Cyclone." My ears perked at the words. Snickerdoodle Cyclone was a shake on the menu at Sip & Shake, and it was delicious. "This place is completely lame."

Something in the girl's stuck-up tone struck a chord with me, and I blushed uncomfortably. Hadn't I basically been saying that exact same thing since I arrived here? Only, surely I hadn't sounded that cruel. I shifted my feet, swallowing thickly. But—oh—what if I *had*?

Wren was frozen behind the register, her furrowed face a grenade about to explode. I stepped instantly to her side, smiling at the scowling teen.

"You're right," I said to the girl. "We don't have Snickerdoodle Cyclones. But I'll make you something even better."

Wren elbowed me. Through her clenched teeth, she hissed, "You're not going to try something crazy like you did with the Lesters. That was a disaster—"

"It'll be fine," I assured her. "You'll see." I smiled at the teen, who was glowering at us with arms crossed. "Go ahead and have a seat. I'll deliver your shake to you shortly."

"Bria . . ." Wren warned. "Bria, wait—"

But I was already out the creamery door and running for the house. A vision for a new shake was forming in my mind, perfectly peaked with whipped cream and a tower of mouthwatering ooey-gooey chocolate of all kinds. I knew exactly what I needed from the house. I just had to hope it was still there and that Luke and Gabe hadn't scarfed what was left of it.

When I reached the kitchen, I smiled. There it was—the

half-eaten tray of Uncle Troy's everything-but-the-kitchen-sink brownies. It was his specialty—something he'd baked for his squadron back when he was younger and had been deployed overseas for months at a stretch.

"I used to throw everything I could think of into the batter," he'd said last night when I'd asked him why he was tossing handfuls of broken pretzels into the brownie mix. "We'd get care packages from home, and everybody would contribute stuff."

These brownies had pretzels, toffee, white and dark chocolate bits, mini marshmallows, and even chunks of Oreo cookies. They weren't necessarily the prettiest brownies on the planet, but—oh my gosh—they were *good*. I grabbed the tray from the counter, and then rummaged through the pantry and fridge, taking anything else I found that would work. With arms overflowing, I hurried back to the creamery.

This time, I started the crazy shake with three scoops of chocolate ice cream, a splash of milk, and a hefty scoop from the jar of hot fudge I'd unearthed from the fridge.

As she took orders, Wren threw me concerned backward glances every few seconds. I knew she didn't want a repeat of what had happened with the Lesters. I didn't want that, either.

Everyone was already so unhappy with me, I didn't want to make it worse.

I plunked a square of brownie into the metal tumbler alongside the other ingredients, then set the mixture into motion with the shake agitator. Once the tumbler filled with thick and creamy chocolatey yumminess, I poured it into a glass. After squirting a swirling dome of Reddi-wip on top, I sprinkled on some chocolate chips, toffee, Oreo, and pretzel bits. That's when the real fun started. I skewered another brownie square and stuck it into the shake so that the brownie hovered over the top of it. Then, on a second skewer, I made a kebob, alternating marshmallows with caramels, Oreo cookies, pretzels, and caramel popcorn pieces. I added that to the shake and, as a final touch, wedged two more Oreos onto the side of the glass.

Just as I finished the shake, Aunt Beth breezed out of the kitchen precariously balancing two trays towering with burger baskets. She took one look at the shake in my hands and stopped cold.

"Don't worry!" I blurted before she could even open her mouth to protest. "It was a special request."

Heaving a world-weary sigh and closing her eyes for a long second, as if she were silently willing the shake to disappear entirely, she nodded. With that reluctant blessing, I carried the shake to the teenage camp counselor. Her head was bent over her cell phone, and she was so consumed in her round of *Candy Crush* that she barely even noticed the shake when I set it down in front of her.

Rude, I thought.

But what I said was, "Here you go." I'd been brainstorming the whole time I decorated and added, "It's a Maniacal Mudslide."

That got her attention at last, and she glanced up. She brightened immediately, but as she studied it asked, "Pretzels?"

I kept my smile firmly in place. "For a sweet and salty combo."

Tentatively, she took a sip. There was a long pause and, finally, the shake won out over her temptation to nitpick. She sat back and admitted, "It's good . . . Really good." I could tell by her second, much longer, sip that it was. A swell of relief and happiness surged through me.

"Hey." Another camp counselor in the adjoining booth twisted around in his seat, ogling the shake. "Where'd you get that? I want one of those, too. It looks awesome."

Across the room, a little girl pointed to the shake, then yanked on her mom's arm, declaring that she wanted a "brownie shake," too.

"I'll see what I can do," I said to the customers as I walked back to the sales counter.

Aunt Beth and Wren were waiting for me.

"No complaints?" Aunt Beth asked warily.

I shook my head. "I have requests for two more."

"We can't," Wren stated bluntly. "I don't even know how to ring those up on the register. And we don't have time—"

Aunt Beth held up her hand for silence. "If Bria wants to make them, she can." Her eyes were on mine, as if she was trying to assess my level of commitment. "You'll have to clean up everything afterward," she told me. "And only make the shakes customers ask for. No more improv. Got it?"

My heart tripped nervously. This was her way of telling me I had one more chance, but I better not blow it. Did I want it? Or did I want to go back to the house for the rest of the day, back to the couch and TV? If I stayed at the creamery, it would mean an endless stream of uber-politeness with all the customers, even the difficult ones, and sore feet at the end of the day. But, crabby customers aside, making the Maniacal Mudslide had been fun. Really fun.

I sucked in a breath, and then nodded with a mixture of excitement and trepidation. "Got it."

"Okay, then." Aunt Beth gave me the first genuine smile I'd seen from her in two days. Wren only nodded briskly and turned back to the line of customers.

I'd made one great shake, but that didn't mean I was off the hook with my family. Still, the Maniacal Mudslide was a start.

"I don't believe it." Aunt Beth stared at the numbers on the page before her. "Sixty Maniacal Mudslides sold. In under six hours."

I was so tired after being on my feet all day that I'd been yawning my way through dinner. But I looked up from my food and noticed, for the first time, that everyone's eyes were on me. Even Gabe, who'd stayed for dinner, was looking at me in surprise.

"So . . . that's good?" I asked.

"It's fantastic." Aunt Beth sat back in the kitchen chair, a mystified smile on her face. "That's more shakes than we sell in an entire week!"

Uncle Troy held out his hand to me for a fist bump. "My niece. Rocking the Dawson milkshake. Love it."

"Thanks, Uncle Troy." A sudden pride welled inside me, catching me off guard. "But it was no big deal. I drink shakes like that in Chicago all the time, but I don't really know much about making them. I sort of winged it."

"Well, I thought it looked professional." Gabe gave me an approving grin. "And it was the best shake I've ever had."

My brow furrowed. "When did you try . . . ?"

He shrugged mischievously. "Luke and I might've grabbed two off the counter when nobody was looking."

Aunt Beth pretended to smack the backs of both their heads. "You sneaks!"

Luke cracked up into his sleeve while Gabe smiled sheepishly. Wren was the only one who didn't laugh. She'd been quieter than usual during dinner and hadn't said boo about my Mudslides.

"You should make more of them," Gabe said to me. "Tomorrow." He looked at Aunt Beth. "They really are cool-looking. I bet more people would buy them."

I blushed at the compliment, and let my hair hide my face.

"Hmm." Aunt Beth looked at me hesitantly. "Would you want to make more, Bria? Today might've been a fluke, but we could try again—"

"Yes," I blurted, before I'd even had time to think. Suddenly, my exhaustion disappeared, replaced by a buzzing excitement. "I'll make more."

The steady flow of customers and the constant requests for Mudslides had made the hours at the creamery fly by. But it was the shake itself—the designing of it and the experimenting with it, making it look its yummiest—that had been the best part of all. When I'd seen customers snapping pics of the shakes—*my* shakes—with their phones, a warm satisfaction had washed over me.

"Maybe I can try some other flavors?" I suggested. "I could do one with s'mores, maybe, and one with Reese's Pieces . . ."

Aunt Beth laughed. "Whoa, whoa. Let's take it one day at a time for now, okay? First, let's see how the Mudslide does tomorrow. But . . ." She gave me a peck on the forehead. "I'm not saying no. Just a 'We'll see.'"

"Okay." Then an idea struck, and my adrenaline surged. "Do you have some colored pencils I could use?"

"We keep all the craft supplies in the cabinets in the mudroom," Uncle Troy said. "Help yourself."

So, while everyone but Aunt Beth and Gabe settled on the couch in the den for TV, I went into the mudroom in search of the art supplies. I only noticed that Gabe had followed me into the room when I stretched onto tiptoe to reach for the case of colored pencils, and he stepped beside me, with a soft "Let me."

He reached past me, his arm brushing against mine for a split second. The warmth of his skin made my pulse leap. He smelled of freshly mowed grass and sunlight, like the outdoors. I was surprised how much I liked it. Even more surprising was that he was here beside me in the first place, when, for the last two days, he hadn't said a single word to me. Or even looked in my direction. I'd thought he hadn't wanted anything to do with me after our talk, but now, here he was, offering to help.

"Thanks," I managed breathlessly when he set the pencils in my hands.

He nodded. We stood there for a moment, unmoving. I waited, not just because I sensed he wanted to say something more, but also because—strange as it was—I liked being so near him, and the way the rest of the world suddenly seemed to fall away under his steady gray gaze.

"Congrats on your shakes going over well today," he started.

I shrugged, blushing furiously once again and hoping he wouldn't notice. "It accidentally happened to work. I mean, I wanted it to, but I didn't know for sure—"

"I know," he said. I felt a wave of relief seeing his smile. It had only been two days, but I realized now that I'd missed it. "It was still a help."

"Did you like it?" I asked. "The Mudslide?"

His eyes lit up and my breath hitched in my throat. "It *was* really good." His voice lifted with his smile. "But for future reference, I'm partial to mint chocolate chip and York Peppermint Patties."

I tilted my head at him and feigned a shocked look. "Oh, making special requests now, huh? So demanding."

"Nah. Consider it a challenge. I wanna see what sort of shake you can sculpt with those ingredients."

"Sculpt?" I rolled my eyes. "You make it sound way fancier than it actually is."

"I don't think so," he said. "Look out, world. Make way for Bria Muller, the next Michelange*la*."

His smile widened, and then I was smiling, too, with a new, unexpected headiness.

"Gabe?" Wren was calling from the kitchen. "Ga—oh." She appeared in the doorway of the mudroom. She glanced from me to Gabe, and the briefest hint of a frown streaked across her face.

"Here you are. We're starting a *Star Trek* episode. I'm making popcorn."

He cleared his throat and took a step back, and it was only in that instant that I realized how close we'd been standing to each other. Without his warmth, I felt the coolness of the air between us.

"Actually, I should head home." He glanced at the clock in the kitchen. "Mom and Dad will be back from work soon."

"Oh. Okay," Wren said.

He moved toward the side door and Wren gave him a disappointed wave, looking like she had something else to say, but it was only "See you later."

He waved back, then gave me a nod and headed out into the night. The moment he was gone, the fogginess in my head cleared, but it took longer for my heart to slow. Wren studied me for a second longer, and then spun on her heel and headed back to the den.

I started to follow, thinking that, for the first time, I'd give one of her Trekkie shows a try to get on her good side again. But my steps slowed when I caught sight of Aunt Beth hunched over a pile of papers in her study, looking worried.

"Aunt Beth?" I peered into the study, and she lifted her head and smiled at me, but not quickly enough to hide the worry on her face. "Is everything okay?"

"Oh, sure." She waved a hand at the papers before her. "Just reading through some paperwork."

Even from the doorway, I could see the CheeseCo logo emblazoned on the pages. "Why do you have CheeseCo papers?"

She smoothed down the pages before her. "I suppose you missed the news yesterday. CheeseCo's officially made an offer now. And it's a good one."

Oh. Well, that explained Wren's foul mood. "So . . . What will you do?"

Aunt Beth gave a tired laugh. "If I knew the answer to that, honey, I wouldn't still be sitting here. Go on, now. Let me stew on these for a bit."

I nodded, sensing that she didn't want me to press any further.

I went upstairs and from the bottom of my suitcase I unearthed the sketchbook Mom had gotten me. Then I returned to the den and sat down on one of the couches with the sketchbook and the box of colored pencils. While Captain Kirk battled a mishmash of alien life-forms, I propped my sketchbook against my bent knees and began to draw.

Ideas for new shakes formed in my minds' eye and, as they did, I put them down on paper. The more I drew, the more lost in my sketches I became. When I finally glanced up, with a crick in my neck and both my feet falling asleep, I realized that the TV was off and the room was quiet. Wren and Luke had gone upstairs. I'd been so consumed with drawing, I hadn't noticed. I glanced toward the kitchen and study and saw that the lights were off. My aunt and uncle must've gone to bed, too.

I stood stiffly and stretched, working out the kinks in my back and legs. Then, with visions of shakes still fizzing and popping in my brain, I dragged myself to bed.

Chapter Nine

I woke to the enticing smell of fresh-baked brownies and sun streaming through the bedroom window. I went downstairs to find Aunt Beth and Wren pulling not one or two, but *four* trays of everything-but-the-kitchen-sink brownies from the oven.

"Second breakfast for Luke and Gabe?" I asked through a muffled yawn.

Aunt Beth grinned. "Your Maniacal Mudslides weren't a fluke."

"What?" I blinked, hazy from oversleeping.

"Word got around in Tillman," she continued. "As soon as the creamery opened, kids were coming in from town asking for your shake. Luke offered them hayrides to tide them over while we made more brownies. But we don't know how to make the shakes."

"Wow." Suddenly I was wide-awake, feeling bubbles of excitement under my skin. "I can't believe it." But then I glanced at Wren more closely, and I saw something else I couldn't believe. I cocked my eyes at her. "Wren, are you—are you wearing lip gloss?"

Her lips had a pearly pink sheen to them, which she instantly tried to hide by awkwardly rubbing the tip of her nose with her hand. But she didn't quite succeed.

"You are!" Aunt Beth declared, with an expression on her face that was a combination of surprise and puzzlement.

"So what if I am?" Wren's cheeks pinked to match her lips.

"What's the name of your crush? Is he over at the creamery right now?" I blurted the words without remembering who I was talking to, auto-shifting into the way that I would've talked to Leila about boys. I instantly regretted it when I was met with Wren's scalding glare.

"This does *not* mean I have a crush," she growled. "On anyone."

Aunt Beth held up her hands. "Won't say another word about it." She pecked Wren on her cheek. "Only . . . you have such beautiful lips. Doesn't she, Bria? Gloss or no."

I nodded, but Wren only rolled her eyes, then scooped up two brownie trays in her pot-holdered hands. "I'm taking these to the creamery."

She was gone before Aunt Beth or I could say another word.

"Always on her guard, my Wren," Aunt Beth said to me. "Never wanting anybody to see her soft spots. I worry how she'd cope with us selling the farm to CheeseCo."

"But . . . I thought you hadn't decided yet."

"Oh, we haven't." She shook her head. "But Mr. Brannigen wants an answer by the end of this week. And he wants contracts signed by July fourth. It's hard to say no to the sort of security CheeseCo can offer . . . Your uncle and I aren't getting any younger. Farm work doesn't get easier."

"Wren told me she wants to run the farm someday," I said. "That would help."

"I can't count on that. And I wouldn't put that pressure on her. Wren has lots of the world to see before she decides." Aunt Beth clapped a hand on the counter. "Well. Enough of that. Why don't you head over to the creamery to give Wren a hand?"

I nodded. What she was really saying, in mom/aunt-speak, was that she wanted me to check on Wren. "Sure."

I found my cousin in the creamery kitchen, scowling down at the tray of brownies on the counter.

"I can't tell if you want to eat them or strangle them," I said teasingly, jolting her from her thoughts.

"Don't," she said, "not after Gabe gave me a weird look on my way over here . . ." She grabbed a napkin and started scrubbing the lip gloss from her lips. "I don't even know what I'm doing," she grumbled. "I *hate* lip gloss! Ick!"

"Wait," I said, "was I right? Is it because of a crush?"

"Don't tell my mom," she pleaded, confirming my suspicions. "Or Luke. He would be so mad."

"Why would Luke be . . ." Luke might tease her for any crush, but he would only be mad if the crush was on someone he cared about. I remembered Wren's frown when Gabe invited me into his rowboat, her short temper whenever she saw me and Gabe alone together. "Is it . . . ?"

"Gabe!" she blurted in a hissed whisper, throwing up her hands. "I like Gabe, okay?" Her voice broke, and she pressed her palms against her cheeks to hide her blush.

How could I not have seen it? I'd known she was upset about CheeseCo, but I remembered her especially upset look when she'd found me and Gabe in the mudroom, standing close. I thought about Gabe's dove-gray eyes, and my stomach dipped confusedly.

"You like Gabe," I repeated. "And . . . you've liked him since . . . ?"

"Pretty much forever," she said glumly.

"B—but you never said anything," I started. "Why didn't you tell me?"

She snorted. "Yeah, because I'm so good at the whole spilling-my-innermost-secrets thing," she said dryly.

"Does he know how you feel?" I asked reluctantly. I didn't want to be hearing this. The whole idea made my palms go clammy.

How could Wren like Gabe when . . . when . . . Oh. My. God. When I liked him, too?

The realization knocked the breath from my body. Of course, I thought he was cute. But it was more than that. He'd gone out of his way to try to help me adjust to this whole new farm life. And he never fell for my "poor me" routine. Sure it was aggravating that I couldn't put anything past him, but it was also refreshing that he told me exactly what he thought all the time. And that I didn't have to try so hard to be perfect around him, the way I did with Leila.

Suddenly, I remembered Wren was there, and I tried to mold my face into a mask that wouldn't give any of my thoughts away.

Wren didn't seem to notice my last-second cover-up. "Does he know how I feel?" she echoed, and rolled her eyes. "What do you think? Telling him would make things completely weird. And he doesn't like me, so what's the point . . ."

"You can't say that for sure if you've never asked him."

"*Bria*. We've known each other since we were babies. He's seen me in diapers, for crying out loud. I just need to get over it." She shook her head. At that moment, Gabe and Aunt Beth walked through the creamery door, and Wren shot me a warning look and hissed, "Forget it, okay? Forget I even said anything."

"Okay," I whispered as they reached us. My pulse surged when I saw that Gabe was holding my sketchbook in his hand. "Hey, where did you get that?"

"I was just down at the house and saw your aunt flipping through it." He grinned.

Aunt Beth nodded. "Your mother always told me you had an artistic flair, Bria, but these drawings are great. Really."

I snatched the sketchbook from Gabe and pressed it protectively to my chest. "They're doodles. I was just playing around."

"They look like more than doodles to me," he said. "They look like the next shakes you should make for the creamery."

"What?" I balked, looking from Gabe to Aunt Beth and back again. "Aunt Beth, I thought you wanted to wait and see."

She shook her head. "Not anymore. Not with the demand we got this morning."

I grinned, flattered that my aunt was willing to give one of my chicken-scratch sketches a try as a legit shake. "But I don't have any of the ingredients I need."

She nodded. "Go on and make a grocery list. You can teach me and Wren how to make those Maniacal Mudslides, and then head to the store. Your uncle's too busy, but Gabe can take you."

"Gabe can drive?" I asked, glancing at him in disbelief. He only smirked mischievously.

"Not a car, no. But he can take you in the tractor."

"Tractor!" I exclaimed. Already, I was picturing a bumpy, dirt-riddled, un-air-conditioned ride. But then I pictured Gabe sitting close to me in a tiny tractor cab, and suddenly, dirt didn't sound so bad. But—oh—then there was Wren. Wren and her crush. Me and my crush. This was a disaster. I looked helplessly at my cousin. She was trying and failing to hide a frown. I forced myself to say, "Maybe Wren should go to the store instead—"

Aunt Beth shook her head. "She's got more experience on the register and in the dining room than you do. Don't worry, Bria, honey." She winked. "You haven't lived until you've taken a tractor ride." She started slicing up the brownies. "Now, let's get this shake how-to underway. Luke will be back from that hayride with the kids soon, and they'll be hot and thirsty."

"I'll see you in a bit," Gabe said to me, and then he was gone.

I was left in the creamery with an even grumpier Wren and a hammering heart. Me, riding in the tractor. With Gabe! The memory of his fresh-cut grass scent hit me, and I gripped the counter. Then I instantly scolded myself. I couldn't be thinking of how nice Gabe smelled. Not anymore.

Gabe didn't like me. He couldn't. He was just a sweet guy trying to help me out. So what if, last night, I'd thought for a moment that he couldn't help staring into my eyes the same way I couldn't help staring into his?

That was last night. Today, I knew that Wren liked him. Today, I knew that Gabe was untouchable. And the tractor ride would surely be just as dusty and uncomfortable as I imagined.

I stared up at the tractor cab, which was much higher off the ground than I'd expected, wondering how I was going to climb into it gracefully.

"Need a hand?" Gabe asked. He was wearing a soft gray button-down that matched his eyes almost exactly, and that bemused look on his face that had totally grown on me.

Wren likes him, I kept having to remind myself. Over and over and over again.

"Nope," I said as coolly as I could. "I've got this." Then, because I'd never actually climbed into a tractor before, I botched the job entirely. I tried to mount the stairs without holding on to the handrail, which I didn't even notice was there until I was losing my balance, scrambling to grab onto it.

I lurched backward, but Gabe's wide hands caught me around my waist, steadying me until I could find my footing.

"Yup, you've got it, all right," he laughed, and I could nearly hear him shaking his head at me behind my back.

I settled myself into the springy seat inside the cab as he climbed into the other side. Once the doors were closed, there was no way to avoid our arms brushing as he started the tractor with a sputtering rumble.

I tried to perch myself as lightly as possible on the seat, hoping if I didn't move much maybe there wouldn't be too many dust marks on the back of my jeans by the time we got to the store.

We pulled out of the creamery parking lot and headed down the dirt path alongside the cornfields, kicking up a cloud of dust as we went. To my dismay, the side windows were open, and I found myself pushing my curls from my eyes every few seconds.

"Aren't we going to drive on the road?"

Gabe shook his head. "I can't until I'm fourteen. Iowa law. So we have to go the back way through the fields to get to town."

"Can we close the windows?" I asked, trying to hold my hair back, but Gabe only shook his head nonchalantly.

"I like the fresh air" was his aggravating response as he watched me, apparently amused.

One of my curls blew into my mouth and I spat it back out, sputtering.

"Close the windows!" I cried. *"Please."*

"Okay, all right," he agreed, and shut the windows. Without the constant breeze, the inside of the cab suddenly felt too quiet.

"Thank you," I mumbled, fighting to tame my curls with a hair band.

"Your hair looks fine," he said, noticing my efforts and frustration. "I like it like that."

My fingers stopped fidgeting with my curls. "Like what? A natural disaster?"

His laugh was solid, warm, and as full of sunlight as he was. "Just . . . natural." The tractor shifted into a lower gear and the engine settled into a steady purr. "You don't have to try so hard all the time, you know."

"What do you mean?" I smoothed out my shirt.

"I mean to be so styled. So . . . put together."

"You don't like my clothes?" I asked.

He shook his head. "Your clothes are cool. You wear so many different colors all at once. It's like . . . you're a living, breathing kaleidoscope." I wasn't sure how to take that until he leaned toward me, laughing. "That was a compliment," he whispered.

I twisted one of my curls self-consciously. "Thanks. I like making unlikely matches." He grinned, and I nearly gasped as the double meaning of what I'd just said sank in. "I mean . . . I didn't mean . . ." Oh boy. Who knew what I meant anymore. I swiftly changed the subject. "My friend Leila, back home, she says that good hair and outfits can make or break an entire social life."

"And you buy into that?" I could tell he thought it was ridiculous.

I sniffed. "She's one of the most popular girls in our school, so . . . yeah. I do."

"Popular," he repeated. "What about nice?"

"Of course she's nice." My voice was tight.

"To everybody?" He glanced at me, waiting. "Or to everybody she thinks is important enough?"

I squirmed in my seat as a memory swept through me. The one and only time I'd asked Leila about including Jane and Devany at our lunch table, Leila had shrugged. "You can eat with whoever you want, Bria," she'd said offhandedly. "You don't need my permission. I'm just surprised." She'd glanced toward Jane and Devany in the lunch line, taken in their outfits, and pursed her lips. "I thought you'd outgrown them."

The idea that I'd ever outgrow my two best friends had seemed impossible, right up until that moment. That afternoon, as I sat down beside Jane in math class, I'd taken in her outfit the way Leila had, and I'd found myself frowning, too, seeing the flaws I'd never noticed before. I never sat with them at lunch again.

Now I felt Gabe watching me, and I wondered if he could see my shame. "Look," I started. "You don't know anything about my friends, so—"

"You're right," he interrupted. "I'm sorry. Sometimes I jump to conclusions. Not fair, I know. It's just, my sister has a friend kind of like your Leila, and—"

"I didn't know you had a sister."

His mouth tightened. "She's older than I am. Twenty. I don't see her very much." He shrugged, as if he wanted to get off the topic. "Anyway, I'll quit with the third degree."

"Thank you," I said, and then we settled into silence. I heard music drifting from the tractor's radio. "You like Pink Floyd?" I didn't even try to keep the surprise from my voice.

His mouth curled into a half smile. "What'd you think, that everybody in Iowa likes country music?" I shrugged, to which he added, "Does everybody in Chicago like the band Chicago?" That made me bust out laughing, and his lopsided smile widened into a proper one. "See? Sounds ridiculous, doesn't it?"

"I guess so." I tilted my head at him, scrutinizing him purposefully and dramatically. "No, I can see how you'd like Pink Floyd. You've got the whole dark-side-of-the-moon personality thing going on."

He raised an eyebrow. "How's that?"

"You act so easygoing all the time, but then you've got this serious, deep side, too." Then I snapped my fingers. "Hey! If you were a shake, you'd be the Dark Side of the *Spoon*."

He huffed a laugh. "Do all city girls make such awful puns?"

I mock-glared. "I don't know. Do all country boys make such awful night-fishing partners?"

He laughed again. "I probably should've warned you about the leeches."

"You think?"

"Then again, seeing you swim for your life is something I'll never forget." He winked. "You might've broken a speed record."

I smacked his arm playfully. "I think you just wanted to see me squirm."

"Maybe a little," he admitted. "Or maybe I was hoping you'd swim off the prima donna attitude."

I smacked him again harder, huffing. Then, after a second, I muttered, "Okay. I guess I *was* being sort of a prima donna."

He smiled. After a minute, he said, "You know, you're good at it."

"What? Attracting leeches? Because if that's my true calling, I'm out."

He shook his head. "The shakes."

"Mixing ice cream and brownies isn't hard," I said.

"Not just that. Designing them. The ones you drew in your sketchbook are like real art."

I snorted. "Sure. I'm a regular Picasso."

His gray eyes were trained on my face. "Don't do that," he said softly. "Don't make it sound like it's nothing special. Where did you learn to design stuff like that?"

"I didn't," I said simply. "I've always liked putting pieces together to make something fun, or beautiful. I guess that goes for shakes as well as clothes. There's a feeling I get when something looks right. It's like snapping a last puzzle piece into place, and then, suddenly, the world makes sense."

"It's you, then." He smiled. "Maybe this is your gift."

"Not likely." I stared down at my lap, my heart hammering. I wasn't one of those people who had natural talent. I was a solid B and C student, and, even though I'd taken a few dance classes and had played soccer when I was younger, I'd never really excelled at anything. "Leila's the one with talent. You should hear her voice—"

"I bet Leila can't make a milkshake like you can," Gabe replied.

The tractor pulled to a stop, and Gabe turned off the ignition. I blinked in surprise, wondering why we'd stopped until he said, "We're here."

I glanced through the cab's window at the grocery store, wondering how the time had flown by so quickly. I started to climb out of the cab, but suddenly Gabe was there, his hands sturdy around my waist, lifting me gently down to the ground.

"Thanks," I said breathlessly. I was disappointed when his warm hands dropped to his sides.

"So what's on this list?" he asked as we walked into the store. I let him read through it, watching as his face grew more and more amused. "Red licorice? Twinkies? And . . . gummy worms?"

"The more over-the-top we make the shakes, the better." I turned a corner into the candy aisle. "You can help. Just grab some colorful candy. Taffy, lollipops. Whatever's fun to look at and eat."

"Razzles?" He held up a package skeptically.

I took it and dumped five more packages of Razzles into the cart. "Sure. Pop Rocks, too."

We spent the next ten minutes filling the cart with every kind of candy imaginable, and then grabbed ingredients for more brownies, cheesecake, and cookies, too. Gabe started lobbing bags of candy into the cart like footballs, and even had me try to catch some passes. It was fun, even if I kept missing. By the time we were done shopping, the cart was overflowing with all things sweet.

"A little early for Halloween, don't you think?" the cashier quipped as she rang us up.

I laughed, inspiration striking. "Stop by Dawson's Creamery for a Towering Trick or Treat shake," I told her. "Available starting tomorrow!"

"Is that even a real shake?" Gabe asked while we pushed the heavy cart out to the parking lot.

I grinned. "It is *now*."

Five minutes later, we were rumbling back down the dirt path and I was busily sketching a design for the new shake on the back of the grocery list.

"That's a first," Gabe said.

"What is?" I asked absently, still focused on my drawing.

"Seeing you so happy. You've pretty much been frowning since the second you got here."

"That's not true . . ." I started to protest. I glanced up from my sketch. "No . . . it's true."

He nodded, satisfied with my admission. "For the record, I like artist Bria way better than stuck-up Bria."

I gave a short laugh. "Are you saying I *was* stuck-up?"

He gave me a sideways look that made my heart tap dance. "How about we say that you're a work in progress?"

I feigned annoyance, but couldn't help smiling. "Like my shakes, I guess." I shrugged my shoulders. "I'll take it." Then, because I wanted to try to get him to understand my perspective, I added, "The thing is, I didn't want to spend my summer here."

He nodded. "I picked up on that the very first day. But . . . why?"

I hesitated, suddenly wanting to tell him the entire story, but worrying about what he'd think of me if I did. "If I tell you, can you promise not to get on my case about it?"

He thought this over, then nodded. "Deal. No judgement."

So I told him about everything that had happened with Jane and Devany and with Leila's YouTube videos. I even told him what I hadn't told anyone else: how I'd unknowingly helped Leila include Jane's outfit in the video. The entire time I was talking, he didn't say a single word. I didn't even dare to look at him, for fear of whatever anger or disappointment I'd see on his face. When I was finished, I sat back, deflated, wondering if he'd break his promise and launch into a lecture about how wrong I'd been.

He didn't. Instead, he said simply, "So? What next?"

"You mean with Leila? Or Jane?"

"Both, I guess." He kept his eyes straight ahead, focused on the path.

"Everything stays the way it is." I swallowed. "Why should anything change? Leila and I are best friends, and Jane and I . . ." My heart dipped. "We're not anymore."

We rode in quiet for a few minutes and then he spoke again. "I mentioned my sister before." His voice was low and sad. "Grace moved to New York City a while ago, and now we only see her once a year, if we're lucky. My parents hate that." He ran a hand over his hair. "My dad was a bull rider when we were younger. He competed in rodeos. My sister didn't like it. She was always scared he'd get hurt. Then . . ." He sighed. "Dad got hooked by a bull and broke his collarbone and one too many ribs. It took him a while to heal, and my sister was so mad at him for letting himself get hurt.

I think she blamed our life here, too. She never liked how tiny Tillman was. She felt limited by it." He shrugged. "Dad thinks she's embarrassed by us and the fact that we choose to live here."

"Is she?" I asked.

"I think, for her, it was more about living someplace with more people like her. Like us." A lock of his hair fell into his eyes, masking his expression. "She didn't like the way she stood out here."

I struggled with what I might say to make him feel better, but when I offered up "Maybe she just felt more at home in the city," I knew from his instant frown that I'd missed my mark. "I'm sorry," I added quickly, "I didn't mean—"

"Just do me a favor." He gestured toward the waving cornfields outside the window. "Take it in while you're here. All of it. And I don't mean just going through the motions. I mean, *really* seeing it, smelling it. Maybe you'll find a reason to change your mind about this place."

"Like what?"

He stopped the tractor in the creamery parking lot, and turned to face me with that irresistible smile of his. "I don't know. You tell me what it is when you find it."

We climbed out of the cab and unloaded the groceries. All too soon, he was walking away to tend to the afternoon chores, offering me one last smile before he disappeared around the corner of the milking barn. I stared after him, wondering what—in these never-ending fields of green—I might find that could possibly change my mind about country living. But more than that, wondering how I could keep myself from falling head over heels for Gabe. I'd worried that it might be hard, but after our tractor ride together, it could end up being impossible.

Chapter Ten

It was still dark outside as I pulled the last tray of double chocolate fudge cookies from the oven. I stood back, surveying the baked goods on the kitchen counter. There were three batches of brownies, cinnamon rolls, four dozen cookies in three different varieties, and two pans of cheesecake bars.

I yawned and glanced at the clock. It was four thirty in the morning. That was just enough time for the last batch of cookies to cool and for me to blend the shakes before everyone else woke up. I set to work, building the Towering Trick or Treat shake first. I blended chocolate ice cream with two hefty scoops of peanut butter, then added in Reese's Pieces and Peanut Butter Cups. Next, I added orange and white sprinkles to a peanut butter layer coating the outside of the glass mug, and then topped the shake off with whipped cream, two peanut butter blossom cookies, and a long wooden skewer adorned with candy corn, gummy pumpkins, and more peanut butter cups. I smiled with satisfaction as I took in the crazy appearance of the shake. Then I set it on the kitchen table and began mixing the other shakes—the Raspberry Cheesecake Colossus, the Smashtastic S'mores, and the Cookie Crumble Castle.

There was one last shake I had to make, and I'd just finished topping it with three York Peppermint Patties when Aunt Beth and Uncle Troy appeared. They took one look at the kitchen and their mouths dropped open.

"Surprise!" I swept my hand toward the shakes lined up on the kitchen table.

"You . . ." Aunt Beth couldn't stop staring. "You made all of this? This morning?"

Uncle Troy staggered against the wall, feigning shock. "Beth, call a doctor. Bria's up before ten. Something's wrong with her."

"Very funny, Uncle Troy." I smirked at him, but he only threw me a proud smile. "I thought we could do some taste testing. So we could decide which shakes to add to the menu at the creamery."

Just then, Luke thudded down the stairs with Wren following, and the second he saw the shakes, he whooped. "Yes! Dessert for breakfast! I knew it was only a matter of time before Mom recognized sugar as the fifth food group."

Aunt Beth clucked her tongue at him, but she was laughing. "Bria did this. Isn't it great?"

Now it was Wren's and Luke's turns to go slack-jawed.

"You don't have to look that shocked," I said with a touch of defensiveness. "I know I haven't been helping much lately, but . . . this is something I can actually do."

Everyone was silent then, until Aunt Beth announced, "All right! Let's dig in!"

That was all it took for Uncle Troy and Luke to grab spoons and straws and sit down, ribbing each other good-naturedly to vie for the first taste of the Smashtastic S'mores shake. Aunt Beth opted for alternating between the Cheesecake Colossus and the Towering Trick or Treat, closing her eyes and muttering, "This much sugar is SO wrong, but it tastes SO good."

Wren reached for the shake with the York Peppermint Patties, but I stopped her, handing her the Cookie Crumble Castle instead. "I'm actually saving that last one," I said.

"For who?" she asked.

That was when Gabe walked in the front door, wearing a slate-blue work shirt that made his eyes look like Lake Michigan on an overcast day. My heart tumbled as I held the last milkshake out to him.

"This one's for you," I made myself say.

"You've been busy," he said, taking in the catastrophe of the kitchen, and then the shake in his hands. I'd coated the top of the glass in ganache, then studded it with semisweet chocolate chips and Junior Mints. The shake itself was a blend of mint chocolate chip ice cream (I'd snuck it into the cart at the grocery store yesterday without Gabe seeing), more ganache, and bits of York

Peppermint Patties. I'd stuck some peppermint sticks into it for garnish, too. "Is this what I think it is?" A slow smile spread across his face.

I nodded, smiling back. "The Dark Side of the Spoon."

"Thanks," he murmured, and took a sip, nodding appreciatively. "It's delicious. What's in it?"

"It's a shake shrouded in mystery," I said teasingly. "Nobody really knows for sure."

His smile widened.

Wren hadn't touched her Cookie Crumble and was clearly listening to us. Gabe plopped down beside Luke, who wasted no time in scooping out a helping of the Dark Side of the Spoon for himself.

Wren stared long and hard enough at Gabe's shake that Luke piped up with, "What's the deal with you, sis?" He elbowed her. "Did you wake up on the dark side, too, or what?"

Wren stood up so quickly, she nearly knocked her Cookie Crumble shake over. "I have chores to do," she mumbled, and was out the door before any of us could say another word.

"What was that about?" Uncle Troy asked after Wren had gone.

Aunt Beth stared at the closed front door, worry creasing her face. "This whole CheeseCo deal must have her completely out of sorts."

My chest squeezed. I had a feeling Wren's irritation had less to do with CheeseCo and more with the shake I'd made especially for Gabe. But everyone fell silent at the mention of CheeseCo, and the cheery mood in the kitchen instantly plummeted.

"I'll go check on her," Aunt Beth said. But she paused to give my arm a gentle squeeze. "We'll add these shakes to the menu first thing this morning."

"I can help add them," Gabe said, shooting me a smile. "We can work on it after breakfast."

"Thanks." I grinned back at him.

Aunt Beth pressed a hand against my cheek. "You did good, Bria."

Then she was gone, and the only sound in the kitchen was the gurgling slurp of Luke sipping the last drop of shake. Finally, I'd done something right around here, and to my surprise, I liked the way it felt.

"How does this look?" Gabe perched atop the ladder behind the creamery's counter, positioning the prices onto the letter-board menu.

I took in the plastic lettering. It certainly wasn't anything close to the flashy digital menu at Sip & Shake, but at least my shake names were fun. And maybe the retro look had its own charm. "It looks good. Thanks."

"Thanks? That's it?" He feigned a frown as he climbed down from the ladder. "I thought I might get another Dark Side of the Spoon for all of my hard work."

I rolled my eyes. "Soooo demanding."

"Hey, you should be flattered." He gestured to the bag of York Peppermint Patties on the counter and gave me puppy dog eyes. "Please?"

I shook my head emphatically. "I have to save the rest of the Yorks for customer orders. Can you imagine the disaster if we ran out?"

"Oh, I see how it is." Snatching the bag off the counter, Gabe made for the door, crying jubilantly, "Ha ha! They're mine now!"

I giggled and tried to grab the bag. "Give those back!"

He ducked away, exclaiming, "You'll never catch me!" He skirted around me as I lunged for him again. I missed, and he ran toward the door, but then I jumped, tackling him to the floor.

"Gotcha," I gasped between gulping laughs.

"Ouch," he groaned, but he was smiling. "I guess you're good at football tackles, too."

As I tried to pry the bag from his hands, I started to tickle him, until we were both breathless and laughing on the floor—until I glanced up to see Wren staring down at us.

"Wren!" I leapt to my feet. "We were just . . ."

"Updating the menu," Gabe finished for me.

Wren's voice was clipped. "Mom wants us to update the menu on the creamery website, too." She turned on the ancient computer behind the sales counter. "She wants us to look at it together."

"Oh. Okay." I straightened my outfit and hair sheepishly, while Gabe shot me a sly grin.

He held up a single Peppermint Pattie. "Victory," he said as he popped it into his mouth. I stuck out my tongue at him, but only when Wren wasn't watching.

"Gabe," Wren said then, "Dad's been looking for you. He and Luke need help fixing the milking machine."

"On it," he said, then added to me, "I'm not giving up on that shake, either."

"Not happening," I called after him as he walked out the door, laughing.

Impatiently, Wren said, "Could you focus please? The Fourth of July is next Monday and we have to start stocking up on ice cream and beef patties now so we don't run out during the bash. And now Mom wants the site updated, too. We don't have time for fooling around."

I nodded, mollified. "Sorry." I sat down beside her to look at the website, determined to focus and forget Gabe.

We sat like that, barely speaking, staring at the computer screen, until Aunt Beth walked into the creamery a few minutes later. "How's it going with the website?" she asked.

"Well . . ." I sighed. The creamery's website was dismally out-dated, with simplistic graphics and the most basic of features. "The website needs some refreshing."

"I know it." Aunt Beth pinched the bridge of her nose. "I put it together ages ago, and I meant to keep updating it, but I just haven't had the time . . ."

"I can do it," Wren said.

Aunt Beth laughed. "But, honey, you don't know anything about web design—"

"So? Bria didn't know anything about making shakes, but *she* learned. I can handle this."

I looked at Wren's determined expression and instantly forgave the bitterness with which she'd said my name. With the guilt nig-gling my insides, I had to back her up on this one.

"Wren's right," I said. "She'll be great at the website. Maybe I can help, if she needs it."

I waited, holding my breath, until finally Wren nodded. "We

could start some social media accounts for the creamery," she said. "Post some photos of the new shakes, and get people talking about them."

"Good idea," I said, meaning it.

Aunt Beth nodded slowly. "Well, even if it's just for a little while . . . I think that would be great." Wren and I shared a surprised look—only a little while? I wondered if Aunt Beth was thinking of the CheeseCo offer and if they'd decided anything. Before Wren could ask what she meant, Aunt Beth pronounced, "Bria, we'll just make sure your parents are okay with you helping on this social media project, and then you two can get started!"

Aunt Beth called my parents then and there. When Mom and Dad listened to my excitement through the phone, they quickly agreed to it. I could hear Mom's relief at my eagerness to help with anything.

Soon enough, I was hard at work perfecting the look of the new crazy shakes, while Wren worked on website overhaul and setting up social media accounts for the creamery.

Once the creamery opened, Wren, Aunt Beth, and I had a

system going. Aunt Beth mixed the basic shakes, and then brought me the extra candy and dessert "accessories" to arrange on top of the shakes. I didn't want to let the shakes out of my sight until they looked just right, and there were dozens of shakes that had to pass "The Bria Test," as Aunt Beth started calling it. Even without social media, word had been spreading around town about the creamery's new shakes, and there was a steady stream of customers all day long. Between my shake arranging and Wren's web designing, we didn't have a second to spare.

Time flew. By the time the creamery closed for the day and we all sat down to dinner, we had a revamped website, and Wren had already posted pics of all the new shakes onto the creamery's feeds.

"You two did all of this?" Uncle Troy said appreciatively as he and Luke scrolled through the new website on Luke's phone.

"It was really all Wren," I said, and she gave me the smallest of smiles.

"Not too shabby," Luke said. "You make us look kind of . . . trendy. Maybe you can give me a social media makeover, too. It could work wonders with my love life."

Wren rolled her eyes. "Luke. Seriously? You'll need more than a social media makeover for that."

I laughed when Luke feigned a dagger to his heart, but my laughter was partly from relief at hearing Wren's joke. She'd been quiet all day, but now she was looking over Uncle Troy's shoulder at the new website and smiling.

"I'm glad we added the pics," she said to me.

I nodded. "They look great."

"And we sold another hundred shakes today, too," Aunt Beth said. "Twice as many shakes as burger baskets."

"That's really something," Uncle Troy said as he filled dinner plates and passed them around. "It's just a shame it's happening now, right when we're about to—"

"Troy!" Aunt Beth's voice was jarringly sharp. Wren, Luke, and I all jumped.

Uncle Troy paled, looking guilty. "Oh boy." He let out a low whistle. "If that's not the sound of Pandora's box opening, I don't know what is." He glanced sheepishly at Aunt Beth. "Sorry, hon."

"Sorry for what?" Wren looked from her dad to her mom anxiously. "What's going on?"

Aunt Beth sat quietly for a long minute, staring at her untouched dinner. "We were going to tell you. You seemed so out of sorts to begin with, I thought it might be better to wait a few days." She heaved a sigh, then reached for Uncle Troy's hand across the table. He took hers, giving it a squeeze. "Your dad and I have decided to accept the CheeseCo deal. We'll sign the papers to make it official next week. We're going to sell the farm."

Her words hung in the air like a dense, poisonous fog, sucking the oxygen from the room. A grave silence swept the table, and I glanced from my aunt's and uncle's grim faces to Wren's and Luke's, shrinking in my seat. This was *not* a discussion I wanted to be here for. No way.

But it was too late.

Wren blurted, "Sell the farm?! How could you?"

"It hasn't been an easy decision." Aunt Beth's lips trembled, but her voice stayed steady. "Mr. Brannigen made us a generous offer."

"What did Mr. Brannigen say to you?" Wren's voice was cold. "I bet that vulture said we wouldn't survive on our own if we said no. That CheeseCo would force us out of business either way."

"Mr. Brannigen is right," Uncle Troy said. "This way of life is on the verge of extinction. We've fought it for years, but we can't stand up to the competition from the conglomerates, and, well, we're getting burned out trying."

"What about us?" Wren asked, gesturing to herself and Luke. "You know I want to stay on the farm. Run it someday—"

"You're too young to make that decision right now," Aunt Beth interjected. "You still have high school and college ahead, and who knows what turns your life will take?"

"You didn't even ask us." Luke's interjection was heavy with sadness.

As everyone hung their heads, I wanted to say something to help. I sucked in a breath. "It doesn't have to be a bad thing," I started, my voice ringing with an awkward cheeriness that fell flat in the gloomy atmosphere. "We'd live closer to each other—"

"Why would I want that?" Wren blurted, and then her eyes

widened. "Sorry, I didn't mean that living near you would be bad . . ."

"I know what you meant," I said softly. And I did. She meant that she'd never want to live in a big city. But for a split second, I *had* thought she meant she'd never want to live closer to me—and that stung. It made me realize how entirely at a loss I was in trying to console my cousins, who'd only ever loved living on this farm, when I'd only ever wanted to leave it.

I stood, clearing my throat awkwardly. "I'm . . . going to check on Tulip. I haven't seen her all day."

The entire family's eyes widened, and I knew they could all see through my ruse. *Tulip?* I was sure they were thinking. *When has Bria ever given two hoots about that goat?*

Their surprise only hastened my exit, until I was practically tripping over myself in my rush to get out the door. Before I made it outside, I heard everyone's voices exploding, speaking over one another. Wren's was the loudest and angriest of all.

I hurried through the darkness, grateful when the sound of their arguing faded entirely. Tulip was standing at the fence, waiting, when I arrived, as if she'd already sensed my distress. I climbed over the fence and, before I even realized what I was doing, sat down right in the middle of the goat pen, forgetting all about the muck and hay I was surely sitting in.

Tulip nuzzled my stomach with her head, bleating loudly.

"Well, it *was* a really great day," I whispered, "until it wasn't."

The two of us sat together in companionable silence for a few minutes. As I pet Tulip, I tuned into the other sounds filling the evening air. The crickets' chirping, the gentle rustle of the corn-stalks as the warm breeze blew—the very sounds I'd found grating when I'd first arrived now struck me as rhythmic, comforting. Even lovely. When had I gotten used to them? I couldn't pinpoint a moment, but now they seemed as natural here as the honking horns and chaotic cadence of people had been in Chicago.

Then, above the countryside soundtrack, came the distant strumming of a guitar. My heart quivered excitedly, and I stood, despite Tulip's insistent tugging on my shirt. Slipping from the goat pen, I let the guitar music lead me until I found myself stepping through the open door of the livestock barn. I walked past the old tire swing hanging from the rafters and deeper into the barn. There, in a far corner lit with the golden glow of a battery-operated lantern, was Gabe. He sat on a low stool with his guitar perched on his knee, and at his feet lay a small tawny calf, curled in a tight ball, dozing.

His eyes lit up when he caught sight of me, but he gestured with a finger to his lips to keep my voice down.

"I thought you'd gone home already," I whispered. "You weren't at dinner."

"I was on the front porch ready to come in when the hollering started," he explained. "I figured it was safer to finish up the chores instead." He glanced at my shirt and pants. "Glad to see you've finally made your peace with mud." A smile played at the corners of his mouth.

"Wha—?" I glanced down and saw tracks of mud on my pants, and the spot where Tulip had made neat work of fraying my shirt's hem. "Oh." I laughed quietly. "I was in the goat pen."

"Since when do you willingly visit the goat pen?"

"Since tonight, I guess." I shrugged sheepishly. "Tulip's not such bad company, except for her manners." He gave a hushed laugh, and his cheeks glowed in the lantern light in a way that made my pulse hammer. "Since when is serenading baby cows one of your chores?"

"She hasn't been nursing." His voice was low and soothing. "I've been trying to bottle-feed her, but she's too nervous. I thought maybe the music would help."

"Want some company?" I asked.

Wait . . . what? Had that actually just come out of my mouth? This was *not* good. It would probably make things worse with Wren if she found out I was hanging one-on-one with Gabe. I turned for the door and, with a jittering heart, I quickly backpedaled. "Forget it. You're busy, and I—"

He caught my hand, and I froze. "Bria." His eyes were soft. "Stay. Please."

"O-okay," I squeaked. My face was burning, and I only started breathing again when he let his hand slide from mine.

"I'd avoid going back to the house for at least a half hour. Maybe more." He picked up the large bottle of milk beside his stool and gently lifted the calf's head, then tried running the tip of the bottle around her mouth to see if he could get her to drink. The calf turned her head away, refusing. "What's the drama anyway?"

"My aunt and uncle decided to sell to CheeseCo," I answered.

Gabe looked up, eyes wide. "Oh wow. I mean, it's not a huge surprise, but it's . . ." As he tried, again, to get the calf to take the bottle, he simply ran out of words. I nodded, understanding.

"There's nothing I can do to help," I confessed. "I don't know the right things to say . . ."

"Because you can't imagine wanting to living here in the first place."

Did I still feel that way? I wasn't really sure anymore. I sank to my knees beside Gabe's stool and the poor, bleating calf. I stroked her velvety neck, and she instantly quieted.

"Look at that." Gabe smiled. "She calmed right down for you."

I laughed softly as the calf stuck her nose against my palm, and then Gabe was handing the bottle to me.

"Give it a try," he suggested. "She might take it from you."

"But I don't know what I'm doing!" I countered, trying to push the bottle back into Gabe's hands. "I can't—"

Gabe settled down beside me, his shoulder pressed against my back. "You can," he whispered. Then, slipping his hand over mine, he helped me guide the bottle toward the calf's mouth. I stroked under her chin with one hand and gently coaxed her into accepting the bottle. Within seconds, she was swallowing the milk with smacking, suckling sounds, her bright brown eyes trained on my face.

"She's drinking!" I laughed. "Good girl. You drink it all down now."

I glanced at Gabe, who was smiling at me, and I suddenly realized how close his head was to mine. Our eyes locked. His hand was still over mine, and my skin was crackling with electricity.

I dropped my eyes a second later, and Gabe cleared his throat and let his hand fall to his side. He stood and turned his head away from me, rubbing his neck.

It only took a few minutes for the calf to finish the bottle, and then Gabe put her back in with her mother for the night.

"You're a natural," he murmured as he latched the stall door.

I shook my head as we walked out into the night air. "I'm not a natural at anything."

Gabe cocked his head at me. "Bria, you're doing it again. Don't discount yourself. Just say 'thank you.'"

I smiled. "Thank you," I whispered, looking everywhere but at him. Finally, my eyes settled on the house. The lights downstairs were all off, and the only remaining light came from Wren's bedroom window. For a second, I thought I saw her silhouette, looking out. Then she was gone.

"I should get inside," I said.

He nodded just as the headlights of a truck turned into the creamery parking lot. "That's my dad," Gabe said. "I have to go. See you tomorrow."

I nodded reluctantly, hating for him to go, but he was already striding toward the truck. As it pulled out, I looked after the taillights, wondering what he was thinking right now, and wondering if one of his thoughts might be about me. Because, as I made my way inside and up the stairs to bed, I was thinking about him, of the way our hands had intertwined, and the way my heart danced when they had. But when I saw Wren's sleeping form in her bed, guilt crashed over me. *No*, I reminded myself. *Gabe is off-limits.* No matter how adorable he looked, no matter what he did or said, I would keep him at arm's length, as a friend and *only* a friend.

Chapter Eleven

The next morning, as I walked into the barn alone, Gabe's surprised face somehow made him look even cuter.

"Where's Wren?" he asked.

When Uncle Troy had come in for wake-up call, Wren hadn't bounded out of bed with her usual enthusiasm. Instead, she'd pulled the covers over her head, leaving me, Uncle Troy, and Aunt Beth stunned. Wren was so tough, and if I was honest, I'd spent so much time bemoaning my own predicament here that I hadn't realized just *how* sad she would be about her parents' decision. But her sniffles the night before in the dark had proven it, too.

The least I could do was volunteer to take her chores today. Even if that offer had left my aunt and uncle double-stunned.

Now I explained, "She's just sleeping in."

Gabe seemed to understand, but then asked teasingly. "You're not actually going to do chores, are you?"

"I heard dirt is a great exfoliator," I responded.

I'd seen in Aunt Beth's face how grateful she was to hear I would help out. And I'd realized I wasn't even dreading heading down to the cows and the dirt and the fresh, cool morning air. Somewhere between serving up shakes and helping that nursing calf, I'd let my guard down. And when I stopped thinking about what Leila might think, and how different everything was from Chicago, I found myself enjoying something I never thought I would have.

I pushed up my sleeves and held out my hands to Gabe. "Now give me one of those milk-suction thingamajigs and stand back. I'm ready to take on the job, hooves and all."

The first three times I tried prepping a cow for milking, I failed, but soon enough, I got the hang of it. It wasn't even close to as bad as I'd originally thought, and the cows were very patient with me, even when I made mistakes. And Gabe's steady presence behind me gave me an extra boost of confidence.

As I pet one of the cows and listened to Gabe strumming his guitar once again, a new resolve settled over me. Today, I silently vowed, I wouldn't utter a single complaint. Today, no matter what awaited me, I'd give this farm my all.

I balanced the tray bearing five Smashtastic S'mores shakes as I wove past the customers waiting at the sales counter.

"I'll be back in just one second to take your orders," I promised them, but the line was getting longer even as I spoke. Without Wren helping at the counter, we were falling further and further behind.

In my hurry to deliver the shakes, I bumped one woman on the shoulder, and suddenly, my entire tray began to tip.

"Watch where you're going," the woman snapped.

I gasped and tried to right the tipping shakes, but then there was a second pair of hands under the tray, rescuing me and the shakes.

"I've got you," Gabe said.

"Omigod, thank you." I gave the scowling woman an apologetic smile, then whispered to Gabe, "She was almost wearing it."

He nodded, whispering back, "With her attitude, maybe she deserves to."

"Shhhh." I giggled as he helped me deliver the shakes without spilling a drop.

Aunt Beth gave us both a satisfied nod as we returned to the sales counter triumphantly. She pulled me aside and murmured, "Thanks for filling in for Wren today, honey. It's a big help."

"No problem," I said, hoping she heard my sincerity.

"Wren's taking this really hard, but I hope she'll be okay," Aunt Beth mused.

I paused, but decided to say, "It's just that this farm is all she's ever known. Kind of like me and Chicago."

Aunt Beth squeezed my hand. "I think you're right. But it's not so terrible being here for the summer, is it?"

For the first time, I tuned into the eagerness in her voice. For the first time, I *really* saw how much it meant to my aunt that I feel welcome here, and how much she wanted me to enjoy myself.

I hugged her. "Don't worry, Aunt Beth. I think it might be growing on me."

Her arms tightened around me. "I'm so glad. Because . . ." Her voice cracked. ". . . this will be your last summer here." My heart dropped as Aunt Beth straightened, subtly swiped at her eyes with the back of her hand, and turned to the ever-growing line at the sales counter. "For now we have work to do! Gabe, how do you feel about helping Bria make shakes?"

"What?" I asked. "Isn't he supposed to be giving hayrides?"

"Not anymore," Aunt Beth said as Gabe slid an apron over his head. "We need more help in here than we do outside. Your uncle's taking over the burgers, and I'll cover the register and bring food to the tables. You two are on shake detail until the crowd dies down. Okay?"

Gabe nodded happily, and my pulse tap-danced. It would take us hours to get through the afternoon rush. Hours where I'd be working side by side with Gabe. My heart squealed a jubilant *YES!* even as my mouth forced out a nonchalant "Okay."

Aunt Beth was already taking the next order.

"So . . . where do we start?" Gabe fiddled with the shake machine, peering into the stainless steel tumbler.

"We've got five more orders for Maniacal Mudslides, so we'll need the chocolate ice cream," I said, trying to remain businesslike. "Three scoops into each tumbler, plus a half a cup of milk. Then drop in some brownie chunks."

"No problem," Gabe said. While Aunt Beth headed for the dining room with a half dozen burger baskets, Gabe scooped the ice cream and splashed in the milk. He glanced at me with an adorably confident expression. "And then I stick the tumbler under this whisk-stick thing and push the butto—"

"Wait, don't—" It was too late. The agitator whirred across the surface of the ice cream mixture, and ice cream and milk exploded from the tumbler, spraying globs of chocolate iciness all over my face and hair. I shrieked and held up my hands against the spray as Gabe frantically hit the OFF button.

I wiped chocolate sludge from my eyes and opened them to see Gabe peeking at me sheepishly. "Whoa . . . um . . . sorry?" He tilted his head at me, then whistled under his breath. "Um . . . you might've gotten a little bit in your hair?"

"A little bit," I mumbled, licking the chocolate from my lips. "A little bit?!" I repeated, louder. His eyes widened, and worry flashed over his face, until I burst out laughing. "I'm covered in goop! You're supposed to put the agitator all the way into the tumbler before turning it on."

His mouth formed a perfect O. He muttered a quiet "Whoops," and then he started laughing, too, and soon, neither of us could stop.

"Hey, how was I supposed to know?" he said between laughs. "I never said I'd be good at making shakes."

"No kidding." I caught my breath at last. "Now I know why you stick with cows."

"Funny." He flicked another fleck of shake in my direction, but I dodged it, then lobbed one of my own, which landed smack on his nose.

"Gotcha!" I cried, but Gabe grabbed me around the waist before I could launch a second attack. I spun around in his arms, and found my face inches from his. Our eyes locked, and then, like the unstoppable pull of two magnets, our lips were moving toward each other's . . .

"What on earth—?" Aunt Beth hollered.

I leapt back from Gabe, my heart pounding. My aunt froze mid-step halfway across the dining room and, seeing the chocolatey mess, clenched her eyes shut. "I am *not* seeing that. Nuh-uh. The next time I turn around, that's going to be cleaned up. Understood?"

Gabe and I nodded even as we stifled embarrassed giggles. Then, as Gabe began wiping up the mess, I hurried to the safety of the bathroom, where I could rinse the shake from my hair and try to make sense of what had just happened. Had it been an almost-kiss, or had I just imagined his lips moving toward mine? I pressed my fingertips to my lips, smiling. I'd wanted to kiss him. But had he wanted to kiss me, too?

No! I scolded myself. *No! No! No!* That never should have happened. Today was about helping Wren, and that meant staying clear of Gabe.

The ridiculous smile fell from my face. I made my way back to the shake machine, vowing no more flirting. And definitely *no* almost-kissing.

When I reached Gabe, he'd already made a second attempt at blending the shake, and this time he'd gotten it right.

"There might be hope for you yet," I teased, and soon we were working side by side in a steady rhythm. I showed him how to decorate the outside of the shake glasses with icing and candies, but quickly realized that I was too much of a perfectionist to let him help. So he took over the shake machine while I accessorized.

Before I realized it, the afternoon rush was over and the flow of customers had slowed. As Gabe and I made the final shake of the day, we talked about how he wanted to work with animals when he grew up and how his dad had taught him to play guitar. When he asked me what I loved to do, I hesitated.

"If you'd asked me that a few weeks ago, I would've said social media. Oh, and shopping. I do *love* fashion, for sure . . . I've been thinking lately that I could go into fashion design someday." A slow smile spread across my face as realization dawned on me. "But I really like coming up with ideas for the shakes, too." I carefully placed one more toasted marshmallow atop the Smashtastic S'mores. "Even if it's not fashion, I want to do something artistic. Creating is fun."

He nodded thoughtfully. "Maybe your interests are changing."

"Maybe." I glanced around the creamery dining room, at the remaining customers and their shakes, and I felt proud. I'd made shakes that people couldn't seem to get enough of, and knowing that I'd created something felt good. "I actually like being here. On the farm." I laughed a little. "So . . . that's a change."

"I'm glad." He smiled. "Is it the company?"

My heart flipped. Was he asking what I thought he was asking? It couldn't be. Could it? "Um . . . I . . ." *Yes*, my heart whispered.

"I mean, cows *do* make great company," he added, his eyes sparkling.

Oh. My. God. He meant the *cows*? "The cows." My laugh was an off-kilter garble. "Right."

He laughed. "Bria," he whispered, "that was a joke." His eyes held mine, his cheeks burning bright red in this too-cute way that made my nerves falter. He stepped closer, his grass and sunshine scent making me dizzy. He sucked in air, and his next words spilled out in one long rush. "WouldyougotothemovieswithmethisSunday?"

"Oh . . ." My heart swelled with elation and then a second later plummeted into despair. Gabe was asking me to the movies, which could only mean that he *did* feel the same way about me as I did about him! It was exhilarating and excruciating. How could I say yes when I knew that Wren liked him? But how could I say no when I'd never liked any boy the way I liked Gabe? I wanted to do the right thing, but what if what was right for me wasn't right for Wren?

"Bria?" Gabe said again, this time with an edge of worry in his voice. "If you don't want to, then—"

"No! It's not that!" I blurted. "I do want to go. It's just—" Oh, god, this was torture. I clenched my fists at my sides. I didn't want to hurt Wren, but . . . would I ever have this chance again? And it didn't seem like Gabe had a crush on Wren. Nothing I did or didn't do would change that, right? I took a halting breath, then smiled at Gabe. "Yes. I'd love to go to the movies with you."

Relief and excitement washed over his face. "It's a date, then."

A *date*! A real date! My first ever. I wanted to dance, to sing, to throw my arms around Gabe, and maybe even take another shot at that near-kiss. But, a moment later, I thought I might be sick. What had I just done to Wren?

Maybe she wouldn't take it too hard, I told myself. Maybe she'd be fine. But what if she wasn't? My breath hitched, and it was on the tip of my tongue to tell Gabe I'd made a mistake. But my heart seemed to have a hold on my tongue that I couldn't break. And the next minute, Aunt Beth and Uncle Troy blew in from the kitchen with brooms and mops, ready to close up for the night, and then Gabe was heading out to the pasture to help Luke with the evening milking.

He waved at me as he walked through the door, leaving me

behind with a smile on my face, confusion in my heart, and an ache in my head that only a crush could cause.

"Is that a new shake?" Aunt Beth asked as I placed a final Sour Patch Kid on a skewer. The creamery was just *slightly* less busy than it had been in the last three days without Wren. But I'd found a moment to work on my newest creation: the Sour Patch Surprise, complete with a Sour Patch Kids kebob, Airheads Xtremes bites, and an enormous rainbow swirl lollipop. I wondered if it might tempt Wren out of the house, where she'd been staying and avoiding all of us. I hadn't seen her all day. But I wasn't sure I had the guts to talk to her. Not when I'd been daydreaming about the upcoming date with Gabe . . . and berating myself for ever saying yes.

I was afraid if I so much as looked at her too long, she'd see right through me. I wanted to help Wren deal with CheeseCo, but I was oh-so-torn over whether, and how, to tell her about Gabe.

"It is," I told Aunt Beth now. "I thought we could use a few new pics on the website. Did you see our online traffic has tripled?"

"We'll have to tell Wren." Aunt Beth smiled. "She's still in her room." She frowned slightly.

As if reading our minds, Uncle Troy burst through the creamery door and headed straight for us, waving a piece of paper in his hands. "I have reinforcements! We're ousting Wren from her barracks. Stat."

"Lord," Aunt Beth muttered under her breath, pinching the bridge of her nose. "He's gone into marine mode."

Uncle Troy slapped the paper onto the counter. "The Omaha River City Rodeo. I picked up the flyer when I was downtown last week, but I forgot about it until today." He grinned. "If we hustle, we can be there by five tonight. See the show, and then eat downtown afterward. Huh?" He raised an eyebrow at Aunt Beth, his eyes bright. "*Huh?* Am I good or what?"

My aunt hesitated. "Troy, you know I love a rodeo, but . . . we still have so much to do before the Fourth of July Bash. Luke and Gabe have to prep the corn maze with our patriotic trivia signs— and you still have to remember what you did with the red, white, and blue lights left over from last year."

"I'll find them," Uncle Troy promised. "But Wren *loves* the rodeo."

Aunt Beth gave a tired laugh. "You're right."

"We should go," I said quickly, before I had a chance to second-guess myself. When I got here, I would have rolled my eyes at the prospect of a rodeo. But now I'd do anything to help lift Wren's mood. I'd never expected how good it would feel to be part of the farm's team. "I could even make some coupons real quick to hand out for our new crazy shakes. Maybe a buy one, get one free type of promo for the Fourth of July Bash on Monday?"

Aunt Beth nodded, looking impressed. "Bria, that's a great idea."

"And I've never been to a rodeo, either," I said then. "It would be . . . fun." Oh. My. Gosh. Had I actually just said that? And *meant* it?

I had!

"That's settled, then." Uncle Troy checked his watch. "I'll go tell the boys. I'm sure Gabe will want to come along, too." My pulse skipped at the mention of his name. "We load up and move out at sixteen hundred sharp."

I stood outside the bedroom door, debating. Should I just open the door and pretend like everything is normal, like back when Wren hadn't been in hiding and I didn't have a huge secret? Knocking politely might be even weirder. Instead, I flung open the door with a bright and cheery "Hey, are you getting read—" I swallowed the last syllable down in shock.

Wren whirled around to face me, sheepish guilt scrawled on her face. "I was just . . ." We both glanced at the outfit she had on—a flowy skirt with a bright orange tank top. *My* outfit. "I was only trying it on," she said defensively.

I nodded, trying to stifle my surprise. "It's fine. I'm not mad." I slipped into the room, taking in the pile of discarded outfits on Wren's bed. So, she'd tried on most of my outfits, not just one. Wow. This was a lot more serious than I thought. "If you're looking for something to wear tonight, you can borrow anything you want."

Her guarded expression relaxed a little, and she drooped onto her bed. "I don't have any skirts and I thought . . . well, I thought maybe I'd try something different tonight." Then she mumbled, "Not that he'll notice anyway . . ."

I sat down on the bed beside her, my stomach suddenly flipping with nerves and dread. "Is this about Gabe?" I asked softly.

She picked at her hem. "I just keep thinking that if I do something different, maybe he'll *see* me differently. But it doesn't matter. He'll never look at me the way he looks at you . . ."

"Me?" I squeaked.

She nodded, sagging farther into the bed. "Bria. Come on. The way he looks at you, it's like you're the only person in the room. Are you telling me that you've *never* noticed?"

"Wren . . ." I started, then my voice died as my heart played tug-of-war with my mind. Telling her that Gabe had just asked *me* to the movies would crush her. And there was no way to gently break the news to her, especially after she'd finally opened up to me. Plus, telling her now would only ruin the night ahead for her. I'd tell her as soon as possible, I promised myself. But not tonight.

"It's always hard for me to get a read on Gabe," I replied

carefully. "I'm not ever really sure what he thinks." This felt dangerously close to a lie, but I forced myself to take a deep breath. "First of all, if you want to try something new, it should be for yourself, not just for a boy. Second of all, any boy would be lucky to date you. You drive tractors and can throw hay bales, and those boots make you look like Katniss Everdeen."

"Yeah right." Wren rolled her eyes at that, but I could see the glimmer of a smile. "Look who's talking, Miss Fashionista. You look great in every single one of your outfits. I'd just feel like an imposter wearing them."

I elbowed her. "That's ridiculous. I'm the one who doesn't own a single pair of work boots. On a farm." She snickered. "See? *I'm* the imposter." We laughed, but I could see from her uncertain expression that she still wasn't convinced.

"How about this?" I said. "I pick an outfit from my wardrobe for you to wear, and you do the same for me? We can swap styles for the night."

Wren snorted. "You wouldn't be caught dead in any of my clothes again."

"I've been trying to keep an open mind." I shrugged.

"Okay," she said at last. I grabbed her in a hug, vowing not to let my feelings for Gabe interfere with helping Wren. I hadn't seen her look this happy all week, and I wasn't going to ruin that.

From the dresser, I grabbed the flowered toiletry bag where I kept my nail polish, lip gloss, and shiny eyeshadow creams. I held it open to Wren, proudly displaying the array of brightly colored tubes and bottles. "Welcome to heaven on earth."

Wren winced. "I'm not sure I'm ready for this."

"Come on." I took her by the hand, leading her into the bath-room. "Let's get our glam on."

Chapter Twelve

Everyone was already waiting in Uncle Troy's Suburban when Wren and I finally emerged from the house.

"How do you walk in these things?" Wren hissed as she toddled her way down the stone walkway in my wedge sandals.

"Just own it," I whispered back. "Think catwalk."

"Right now I'm thinking face-plant."

After trying on at least a dozen more outfits, she'd decided on one of my favorite maxi dresses in a royal purple color that set off her fair skin, rosy pink lips, and hazel eyes.

Now I glanced down at the burgundy cowboy boots on my own

feet. "I might never give these back. I can't believe how comfortable they are."

"Don't even think about keeping them," she said with a teasing glare.

Uncle Troy hopped out to open the passenger door for us. "Cinderella," he said with a bow to Wren. "Your carriage awaits."

"Dad. Please," Wren moaned.

"What? I'm not allowed to be awestruck by my daughter's beauty?"

"Not if you don't want an elbow in your awestruck gut," Wren warned, but she was laughing as we climbed into the back of the car.

As soon as Luke and Gabe set eyes on us, they froze, staring.

"What happened to you?" Luke asked Wren.

He was promptly answered with a shove and a muttered "Shut up."

"She looks amazing," I scolded as I took a seat in the far back across from Gabe. I could sense him taking in the cowboy hat, the

Levis, and the glittery red rhinestone snap-button shirt I was wearing—all borrowed from Wren.

"What?" I asked finally, feeling a twinge of self-consciousness. "Is the hat too much?" I dared to look at him. His merrily glinting eyes set my insides fluttering.

"No," he said, "it suits you. You look . . . great."

I blushed. My eye caught Wren's as she put on her seat belt. Her smile had suddenly tensed around its edges.

Uncle Troy bellowed, "All right, troops! Who's ready for a rodeo?"

Aunt Beth whooped, while I asked tentatively, "There won't be blood, will there?"

"That's the best part." Luke grinned.

"What's wrong with you?" Aunt Beth smacked his knee. "Sick."

I shot a worried glance at Gabe, who offered me a heartening smile. "Don't worry. It's like nothing you've ever seen before."

I gave a small laugh. "That's *exactly* what has me worried."

I envisioned ten-gallon hats, bloodthirsty bulls, and belt buckles far too big to be fashionable. *For Wren*, I kept repeating.

I'm doing this for Wren. But when I looked down at my rhinestone-clad shirt and cowboy boots, I wondered exactly what I was in for.

The moment I stepped into the bright lights and immense stadium of Omaha's convention center, I froze.

"Omigod." My eyes swept the packed stands of thousands of people, the dirt-filled center arena, and surrounding bull pens. The crowd gave off an excited hum as country music blasted from speakers overhead, and the scents of deep-fried food, hay, and animals mingled. Dozens of bull riders in boots and chaps were standing around the pens, pinning competition numbers to their backs or adjusting their thick leather gloves.

"I've entered a parallel universe," I said, looking around in amazement. "How is it possible for this many cowboy hats to exist in one place all at once?"

Beside me, Gabe laughed. "I can practically see the fashion police inside you screaming to get out."

"No. Nuh-uh." I shook my head. "Not tonight. Tonight, I'm just going with it. Taking it all in. Every. Last . . ." I gaped as a long-legged cowboy with a belt buckle as big as my head brushed by. "Bit of it," I finished with a squeak.

Gabe nodded, grinning. "I'm going to enjoy watching this."

"Come on, guys." Luke nudged us impatiently. "Let's find our seats and then grab some funnel cakes and elephant ears."

"Some what and what?" I asked blankly.

But Luke was already heading up the stadium stairs, taking them two at a time, with Gabe and Uncle Troy following.

Aunt Beth watched them go, shaking her head. "Bull riding. It turns them positively primal. They'll be grunting over gravy fries and chili dogs in under five, I guarantee." Then she turned to Wren and me. "So, you two are set with the coupons?"

I pulled out the FOURTH OF JULY BASH! BUY ONE SHAKE, GET ONE FREE coupons I'd printed before we left. I'd used one of the best pics Wren had taken of the Smashtastic S'mores shake, and it was eye-popping, if I did say so myself. I tried to hand a stack of coupons to Wren, but she was staring up into the stands, distracted. "Wren?"

"Oh." She blinked and took the stack. "Coupons. Right."

Aunt Beth looked worried, so I stepped in with a cheerful "We'll hand them out and then meet you in the stands in a few. We're good!"

Once Aunt Beth had started for the seats, I turned to Wren. "You okay?" I asked.

She only nodded and busied herself with the coupons.

I did the same, stopping people walking by to hand them a coupon, making sure I dropped the Dawson's Creamery name as I did. I'd handed out dozens of coupons when I spotted an older man and woman walking by wearing press badges clipped to their shirts. The woman had an impressively large camera hung around her neck. I grabbed Wren's arm as adrenaline surged through me.

"Look!" I hissed in her ear. "A reporter and photographer for the *Omaha Gazette*!"

Wren shrugged. "So?"

I stared at her. "So if we can get them to come out to the creamery, maybe the reporter will write up something about our new crazy shakes!"

I yanked Wren toward the reporter with such force that we nearly slammed into him.

"Hi, Mr. . . ." I sneak peeked at his press badge to get his name and got even more excited when I saw that his title was FOOD EDITOR. "Mr. Gilford." I beamed up at him. "My name is Bria Muller and this is my cousin Wren Dawson. Wren's family owns Dawson's Dairy and Creamery in Tillman, Iowa, and we're handing out coupons for our crazy shakes. Buy one, get one free!"

"I see." Mr. Gilford glanced down at the coupon with a smile. "Young entrepreneurs, eh? I don't hear of many family-owned-and-operated farms anymore these days. They're a rare treasure. And I do like milkshakes."

"We have the best," I said confidently, even as I felt Wren shift on her feet beside me.

"Do you, now?" He laughed good-naturedly as the photographer busily snapped pics of some people in the crowd eating corn dogs and cotton candy. "Well, right now I've got to go taste test some of this rodeo food, but it sounds like I'll have to get out to Tillman to try one of your crazy shakes sometime."

"We hope you will!" I called after Mr. Gilford as he moved through the crowd. He waved a final goodbye in return.

"That was so great!" I gushed, but Wren shrugged. Frustrated with her, I focused on handing out the rest of our coupons.

"I'll bet we have a whole new group of customers coming into the creamery for the Fourth of July," I said when we were finished and heading to our seats. Wren didn't answer, but Gabe and Luke hopped up to let us sit.

Luke plopped back down beside Wren, leaving me with the seat next to Gabe. Part of me wanted to offer the seat to Wren, but another part of me wanted to take it for myself. As I waffled over my decision, Wren gave me a fierce look and blurted, "Sit down, already, Bria!"

I sat, feeling a guilty pleasure when Gabe smiled at me. "Hey," he whispered. "How did it go with the coupons?"

It couldn't hurt just to *talk* to Gabe, right? "We gave away the whole stack," I said. I filled him in on our encounter with the reporter, too. "I think we really got the word out."

"Awesome." Gabe held a paper plate out toward me. I peeked

under the piece of parchment paper and found a waffle-like fried pastry doused in powdered sugar. "Your first funnel cake," he explained with a smile.

"I'm a little afraid." I stared at the mountains of powdered sugar. "How do you even eat something like this?"

"Observe." Gabe pulled off a chunk of the pastry and, with powdered sugar showering onto his jeans and shirt, sank his teeth into it.

"Okay, here goes." I pulled an even bigger piece from the pastry and bit into it. It was fried golden crispy on the outside and filled with sweet, chewy doughiness on the inside. "Yum," I said around my mouthful, only getting more sugar across my shirt. We both laughed as I tried futilely to brush it off. "This is unbelievably good."

"A shake in the making?" he asked.

"Definitely. Maybe . . . The Fantastic Funnel?"

"I like it." He pointed toward the arena below, where a cowboy-hat-wearing rider was standing poised over an enormous, restless bull, his feet perched on either side of the pen's railings. "See that rider in the bull chute? Keep your eye on him. He's getting ready to ride. He has to stay on for eight seconds."

"Only eight seconds?" I asked. "That's not very long."

"When you're riding a beast like that, it feels like an eternity. At least, that's what my dad says." Gabe kept his eyes on the arena. "He still misses riding."

"Even though it almost killed him?"

He nodded. "The danger of it is part of the thrill. He's actually here tonight." Gabe pointed toward a group of people standing just beyond the arena gates. "There he is. He's the on-site doctor for tonight's rodeo. Whenever there's a rodeo nearby, he volunteers. It's his way of keeping his hat in the ring."

"I didn't know your dad would be here!" I peered down at the people until I picked out a man in a Stetson hat who was the spitting image of Gabe, only decades older and darker skinned. "I'd love to meet him."

Gabe smiled. "I'd like that, too. We can say hi after the show."

I nodded, then perched on the edge of my seat, watching as the rider cautiously sat down on the bull and strapped one hand tightly around the rope on the animal's back. The moment the rider made contact with the bull, the bull lifted his head, alert and agitated. Then, after a nod from the rider, the gate slid open, and the bull shot from the chute, bucking and spinning, his back legs kicking out behind him violently.

The bull spun faster and faster and the rider slid to one side, and then suddenly fell, landing underneath the raging bull.

I sucked in my breath and closed my eyes, instinctively turning to hide my face, and inadvertently pressing into Gabe's shoulder. "Tell me when it's over," I said as the crowd around us gave a collective gasp.

A few seconds later, Gabe whispered into my ear, "It's over."

I realized his arm had somehow made its way around me, warm and strong. I peeked through my fingers into the arena, where I saw the rider standing and brushing himself off as the bull trotted back into the holding pen.

I straightened. My heart was racing. Gabe's arm slipped away, and we both sat stone still, avoiding each other's gaze.

Another rider settled himself on a bull in the chute. I wasn't sure I wanted to watch, but I *had* to. I gripped my seat and held my breath as the bull and rider did battle in the arena. This time, instead of hiding my face, I cheered the rider on and leapt from my seat to clap madly when the bell clanged to signal the end of a successful eight-second ride.

Soon, I'd eaten my way through three funnel cakes and was enjoying the rest of the show. Bull riding, as it turned out, was only a portion of the night's events. There was barrel racing, where people guided horses at impossible speeds around big blue barrels, and cattle roping, where people swung lassoes at cows and wrangled them to the ground. I was sure Leila would think it was all completely barbaric, but I found it thrilling. By the time we left the arena after the show ended, I was pulsing with adrenaline and energy.

"That . . . was *insane!*" I gushed as we walked through the twinkling lights and cobblestone streets of Omaha's Old Market historic district. "I mean, that bull just flung him around like he was a rag doll. Did you see? And, omigod, the way he hung on . . ."

Uncle Troy and Aunt Beth exchanged smiles, and Wren, Luke, and Gabe all burst out laughing. I stopped midstep to look at all of them.

"What?"

"Bria, don't panic or anything," Gabe started teasingly, then leaned toward me to whisper, "but I think you might like rodeos."

I couldn't deny it. "I do," I agreed, sounding as surprised as I felt. "I *really* do."

Luke gasped and staggered like he was going to fall over from shock, but Aunt Beth looked pleased.

"Look out," Wren said with the first genuine smile she'd had all night. "She's gone country."

I rolled my eyes. "I wouldn't go that far. But I do love these boots."

As everyone laughed, I took in the street before us: the eclectic displays in the shop windows and the old, historic brick warehouses turned into trendy restaurants. Wrought-iron accents graced some of the storefronts and outside cafes where diners mingled, sitting at candlelit tables. It didn't look at all the way I'd imagined. I was surprised to find that I thought it looked . . . cool.

"I'm glad I got to meet your dad, too," I told Gabe. We'd talked with Dr. Reeves before we left, but he'd been busy examining a bull rider with a broken leg, so he'd only had a minute. Even in that short time I'd seen how much alike Gabe and his dad were—both soft-spoken and with a merry kindness in their eyes. "I see where you get your gift with animals from. Your dad has the same gift with his patients."

"He's a great doctor," Gabe said. "And . . . thanks. For saying that. I like the idea of being like him." He smiled at me, and my pulse skipped.

Ahead of us, Uncle Troy pointed up toward a festive-looking steakhouse strung with colored lights. "The restaurant's just up ahead."

We were nearly at the door when I heard someone in the distance, calling my name. Confused, I turned to a shadowy figure waving to me from across the street.

"Bria! Omigod, it *is* you!"

My heart slammed in my chest as Leila—of all people!—stepped out from under an awning and into the light of the streetlamps, making her way toward me with another girl in tow. I was still trying to wrap my head around *Leila* actually being in Omaha when she reached me.

"What are you doing here?" I asked as she gave me a light peck on each cheek. "This is crazy—"

"We're only staying here for one night. We're on our way to Colorado for Fourth of July week." She rolled her eyes. "Family vacation." She mouthed the word *boring*.

"Oh." My tone was surprised. "I . . . didn't know you were going to Colorado."

"Sure you did. *And* I told you we might be driving through Omaha, too. Remember?" Before I had a chance to respond, she added a clipped, "I can see you don't. Way to listen, bestie."

I racked my brain until a vague memory surfaced of Leila mentioning casually that she "might" be passing through Omaha. "Oh, yeah. You did. Sorry. I guess I forgot."

"No biggie." Leila slid her arm around the brunette standing beside her. "Anyway, Chrissie just moved back to Chicago from Paris. Our fams have been close for ages. Her parents have a vacation home in Vail, and our dads are doing a whole hiking, water-rafting thing."

"Oh," I said again, feeling awkward. "Hi," I said to Chrissie, who gave me a curt nod. How had I never heard about Chrissie before? Especially if they were close the way Leila said they were? Despite this, I cleared my throat and smiled at Leila. "How are you? I emailed you a bunch of times, but you only wrote back once . . ."

"Right." She drew out the word. "That's what happens when you don't have a cell phone and can't text. Anyway, what are *you* doing in Omaha? I thought you were still stranded in the backwoods somewhere. On that farm or whatever." She whispered something into Chrissie's ear, and they both giggled.

I shifted uncomfortably, sensing that my family and Gabe were watching us all. "We came into Omaha for the rodeo tonight." I introduced my aunt and uncle and everyone else, but Leila seemed only mildly interested, at best. A moment of awkward silence followed, and then Uncle Troy said they would all wait for me inside the restaurant.

As soon as they started walking away, Leila burst out laughing. "Oh my god, Bria. I feel so awful for you. You're on a farm with nothing to do. And now they're dragging you to rodeos?"

"It wasn't so bad," I started. "And I've been doing some cool stuff at the farm. My aunt and uncle have this creamery, and I've been inventing shakes for them to sell. They're kind of like the ones at Sip & Shake, but my own ideas, and—"

"Wait." She waved a hand to stop me. "First, spending your summer copycatting Sip & Shake shakes is so . . . desperate. And, second . . . I mean, look at you!" She glanced at my outfit. "What are you even wearing?"

My cheeks burned. A little voice in my head reminded me that I'd *wanted* to wear everything I had on and that I even *loved* the boots. But a bigger part of me seized with panic. What had I been thinking? I couldn't tell Leila the truth. She would lump me in with the rest of the "fashion losers" she loved to laugh at, maybe even put me in her next YouTube video. Worse, what if she decided I wasn't worth being friends with anymore? It wasn't like I could go back to hanging with Jane or Devany. Not after how I'd treated Jane.

I swallowed, then blurted, "I wanted to wear it for my cousin. I feel so sorry for her. She has the worst fashion sense, and she's been dealing with some stuff lately, so . . ." I shrugged. "I let her pick out an outfit for me. One of hers." I rolled my eyes, even as a wave of guilt washed over me. "I wouldn't be caught dead in something like this otherwise. You know that."

Leila scoffed. "I wouldn't be caught in it *ever*. But it's your fashion disaster. I guess it's sweet that you let your cousin try, even if she failed. Miserably."

I clenched my fists, hating what she was saying, and—more—hating what *I'd* just said. But Leila was my social lifeline, and I was paralyzed at the possibility of what defying her might do. Desperate to get out of this situation as quickly as possible, I said, "Well, I should get inside. They're waiting for me."

"We should go, too," Chrissie said, in a tone that seemed to say she'd already wasted enough time with me for one night, or maybe for the rest of her life.

Leila nodded and said, "Don't worry, Bria. Chrissie and I will get you back on track before school. After you come home, we'll have some *real* shakes and you can fix . . ." She gestured to my outfit. ". . . this."

She linked arms with Chrissie, gave me one last wave, and walked back across the street. Regret weighing heavily on me, I turned toward the restaurant, and nearly slammed into Wren.

Nausea instantly churned my stomach. Oh no. How long had Wren been there? What had she heard?

"Wren, what are you—"

"Mom sent me out to get you." Her expression was grim and her tone was clipped, confirming my worst fears. "Our table's ready." She spun on her heel and was ten steps ahead of me before I even had time to react.

I scrambled to catch up with her. My heart hammered. "Wren, wait up!" I caught her hand just as we reached the restaurant's door, and she whirled on me, eyes blazing. "Wren, I—"

"Leave me alone!" She spat the words, and I instinctively jerked back from them. "God, I feel like *such* an idiot." She gestured to her outfit. "I dressed up like this, thinking it would make a difference with Gabe. But what's the point?" Her words were flat, cold stones dropping to the ground. "I have the worst fashion sense ever!" Her eyes bored into mine. "Isn't that what you just said? I'm such a horrible dresser that you actually feel sorry for me. I heard every word."

I opened my mouth, but no sound came out. I couldn't argue with the truth. For a second, I thought I might be sick.

Wren's voice wavered between rage and sadness. "I wish you'd never come here."

"Wren," I croaked, finally finding my voice. "I didn't mean it. I swear. You have no idea what Leila's like, how much influence she has."

"Why do you even care?" She threw up her hands. "You said yourself that she's barely emailed you at all this summer. And she was all cozied up to that other girl, when she's supposed to be *your* best friend. What sort of a best friend is she, when she makes fun of you and everyone else you know?"

"I—I . . ." I couldn't think of a single thing to say in Leila's defense. Not right now. "I shouldn't have said what I did, and I—"

"Save it." Even in the darkness under the restaurant's awning, I could see Wren's trembling mouth and welling eyes. "You're no better than she is." She yanked open the door. "You don't care about anyone but yourself."

The door gave a resolute *Bang!* as Wren disappeared behind it, and I was left standing outside, gutted, my own eyes filling. After sucking in a shuddering breath and wiping my eyes, I stepped through the door, wondering how I was going to make it through dinner with my family, when I'd betrayed them all.

I woke up disoriented and with a kink in my neck. It took me several seconds to identify the unfamiliar shadows around me as the lamps, bookshelves, and coffee table of the den. The second we'd gotten back to the farm, Wren had locked herself in the bedroom, so I'd opted to sleep on the couch downstairs. Aunt Beth had tried to find out what had happened, sitting down beside me on the couch after Luke and Uncle Troy had gone to bed. But how could

I possibly tell her? Each time I thought about it, a fresh wave of nausea crashed over me. All I could manage was a wretched, "Wren and I had a fight. But don't worry. We'll figure it out."

If only I believed that were true.

Wide-awake now, I resigned myself to the fact that I'd probably never get back to sleep. Even though it was three thirty in the morning, I flipped on the side table lamp and brought my aunt's old photo albums out from their spot on the bookshelf. I hadn't looked through them before, but now I took my time, pausing over each old photo of my aunt and mom, paying attention to every detail. To my surprise, I recognized so many of the spots where the pictures had been taken. There was the old tire swing in the barn and the front porch of the farm house. There were Aunt Beth and Mom as little girls, sharing a vanilla milkshake, forehead to forehead, at a booth in the creamery. There they were running through the cornfields and riding in the hay wagon.

As time moved on in the albums, there were photos of their weddings, of my grandfather holding me and Wren in his arms as newborns, only a few months apart. We were cousins, but we looked so much alike in our baby pictures, we might've been mistaken for twins. I traced the outline of our toddler faces with my fingertip, my heart aching. How could I have hurt her so badly? And all for the sake of Leila?

What sort of a best friend is she? Wren's words were a haunting echo in my mind.

Suddenly, I was revisiting every one of Leila's snarky comments over the course of our friendship, every subtle dig she made at my expense, every joke she made at someone else's. For so long, I'd thought her remarks about people's outfits were clever and her choosiness over friends a mark of discernment. But now, it was as if a curtain had lifted, and I was seeing her the way other people did. The way Wren had. And probably Jane, too. As snobby, elitist, and hurtful.

My eyes brimmed as a certainty swept through me. I'd been fooled by Leila. Worse than that, I'd been becoming more and more like her. Maybe I'd done something good making shakes for the creamery, but had I been a good friend to Wren in the process? Had I tried—*really* tried—to help her through all the family drama over CheeseCo? Or had I just focused on myself instead?

The wall of tears I'd held back all night broke open, and I started crying. The tears seeped the shame out of me, and once my eyes were parched and tired, a calmness replaced it. As soon as I decided what I was going to do, the weight in my chest lifted a little. Apologizing wouldn't be easy, but I had to try.

Setting the photo albums to the side, I sat down at Aunt Beth's computer and opened my email. Taking a deep breath, I started a message to Jane. Jane, the one who'd still emailed me weeks ago, despite what I'd done to her. Jane, a true, good friend—someone I should never have given up in the first place. *Hi Jane,* I began with trembling fingers.

> *You probably didn't expect to hear back from me.*
> *But I wanted to thank you for emailing me,*
> *especially when I don't deserve it. I also wanted to*
> *say that I'm sorry for the way I treated you over*

the last few months. I'm even sorrier for helping

Leila with her YouTube video. I haven't been

myself, and I hurt you. I see that now.

I'm not sure you want to talk to me, or ever

hang out with me again. But I hope you will,

someday. I'd love to see you and Devany when I

get back to Chicago. Maybe we can try a new

shake place together? The three of us.

Love,
Bria

I sat back, reread the email a few times through, and then, before I lost my nerve, hit SEND.

With the email done, I checked the creamery's website and social media traffic. I wrote down all the stats for the last two weeks. (I knew Wren hadn't been checking it.) A plan was forming in my mind, but I was going to need all the evidence I could muster. I didn't know if Wren would even want to hear my idea, or if she'd ever speak to me again. But again, I had to try.

I didn't want to be like Leila. Not anymore. I didn't want to be like anyone except myself.

And right now, Bria Muller needed to try to make everything right.

Chapter Thirteen

A heat wave swept into Tillman County in the predawn hours, and by the time Aunt Beth, Uncle Troy, and Luke came downstairs, the air inside was sticky with humidity. Still, when Luke asked Aunt Beth why Wren wasn't up yet, I knew it was guilt that turned my palms sweaty.

"She'll be down later" was all Aunt Beth said, but the worried look she exchanged with Uncle Troy only made me feel worse.

I imagined Wren curled into a ball in her bed upstairs, the pile of discarded farming magazines sitting atop her dresser—the magazines she hadn't touched since my aunt and uncle's announcement about selling the farm. My heart squeezed. I knew that there was really only one small way I could start making amends for what I'd said to Leila about Wren—words that were still lodged like splinters in my gut.

"I think I'll wait on breakfast," I said to Aunt Beth as I folded up the blanket I'd slept on the couch with. "I want to get the chores done before it gets much hotter."

"Smart," Uncle Troy said, mopping his brow with a handkerchief.

I headed out the front door and went in search of Gabe. He didn't usually work on Saturdays, but Uncle Troy and Luke had asked for a little extra help getting the farm ready for the Fourth of July Bash.

As I walked through the farmyard, I heard the strumming of Gabe's guitar drifting from the open door of the milking barn. My breath caught, and I froze midstep, second-guessing my decision. Oh, I loved the sound of that guitar. And the boy behind the music was in the barn, the country boy who—against everything I thought I'd wanted—had stolen my citified heart.

But then I thought about Wren's crumpling face, about the

shield she was so good at placing between herself and the world, and how I'd seen the vulnerable girl behind it. Even though it might be one of the hardest things I'd ever have to do, if I stood any chance at gaining back Wren's friendship, I was going to have to forget about my crush on Gabe . . . forever. I stiffened with resolve and walked into the milking barn.

There was Gabe, perched on a stool with his guitar, his hair falling into his eyes. When he glanced up and gave me that charming smile of his, the rest of the world fell away. It only made what I was about to do that much harder.

"Hey, you." Gabe stood up and came toward me, but when he saw the look on my face, his smile faded into a look of concern. "What's the matter?"

My ears filled with my roaring pulse. "I—I need to talk to you." I swallowed, trying to bolster myself long enough to say what I didn't want to, but *had* to, say. "I—I'm so sorry." Each word was a nettle on my tongue. "But I can't go to the movies with you tomorrow."

His smile dropped, and the pink in his cheeks flamed to crimson. "I—I don't understand . . . Why not?" He glanced down at the ground as if he were trying to work through a puzzle. "I already bought the tickets, and I thought that you, I mean, maybe I misread . . ." He lifted his head, and when I saw the bruised look in his eyes, my heart broke. "I thought that—"

"That I liked you?" I finished, forcing my voice into a calmness that my trembling body didn't feel. I kept pushing words out of my mouth, even though each one was wrong. Wrong, wrong, wrong. "I didn't—don't. I'm sorry if I misled you. I didn't mean to." I swallowed thickly.

"You . . . you didn't mean to mislead me?" His normally quiet voice was hardening, growing colder. "So was it some kind of joke between you and your city friends back home? To see if you could humiliate some boy from Tillman?"

"N—no!" I stammered, floored that he would even think such a thing. "It wasn't like that at all."

"Sure it wasn't." He shook his head. "I really believed that you'd changed since coming here. That you'd dropped the attitude for something real. I guess I was wrong." He brushed past me, marching toward the barn door.

"Gabe." Every fiber of my being stung from his words. But he was right, in a way. When I'd first gotten here, hadn't I done my best to try to prove how "above" the farm I was? And now I was paying the price for it. For all of it. "Gabe, wait! Please."

He slowed, then stopped, regret carving a deep trough in his forehead. "What is it?" he asked me.

"I wanted to say . . ." I sighed, knowing I couldn't come right out and tell him about Wren. She was already mad at me now, but she'd never forgive me for revealing her secret. Still, painful as it was, maybe I could drop a hint. "There could be someone right under your nose who likes you. Maybe you've just never noticed."

His brow crinkled in confusion, but then his eyes widened, and I knew he understood who I was talking about. The weight of what I'd done sank in. I'd opened a doorway between Gabe and Wren, and shut myself off from Gabe forever.

"I want you to know . . ." My voice shook. "You . . . you've been a great friend to me. A better friend than I deserved."

And then *I* was the one pushing past *him*, running out the barn door, leaving my heart behind, alongside Gabe's guitar.

I spent the rest of the day at the creamery trying *not* to think about Gabe. I tried *not* to think about his storm cloud eyes or the way his black curls shone in sunlight. I tried *not* to think about how I should've kissed him when I'd had the chance. Mostly, I tried not to think about his kindness, his truth telling, and how much I was missing *him* already.

Instead, I stayed glued to the shake machine, trying to lose myself in the process, hoping that if I stuck with it for long enough, my heart would stop hurting. It didn't. I felt Aunt Beth's worried glance more than once over the course of the morning. But she didn't press me with questions, leaving me to keep my hands busy and my mind occupied. And I was beyond relieved when she told me that Wren (who'd apparently finally gotten out of bed) would be out driving the tractor for the hayrides.

"Taking a breather from each other will do you both good," she'd said breezily.

I knew I needed to talk to Wren, but I still felt too raw.

It wasn't until that night, after an unusually quiet dinner with an absent Gabe and everybody else lost in their own thoughts, that I went in search of Wren. I gathered up my courage, plus the creamery sales figures I'd printed out earlier, and tiptoed upstairs.

After spending the day assuming I'd be sleeping on the couch again, I was surprised to find her bedroom door open. I knocked, then peeked tentatively around the door.

"Can I come in?" I asked.

Her expression was unreadable as she shrugged. "Door's open, isn't it?" Her voice was tired, but void of anger, which I took as a promising sign.

I perched on the edge of my bed with a new awkward politeness. The sadness I felt over losing Gabe tangled with the regret I felt over hurting Wren, until I thought my heart might combust in confusion. I pressed my hands together to steady them. "I . . . wanted to say that I'm sorry."

"You said that already." Wren spoke quietly but bluntly. "Last night."

"This is different." I stared down at the worn floorboards. "I'm sorry about the way I came here, with my snobby attitude. I'm sorry I blew off working around the farm for so long, and that I stuck you with all the chores. I'm sorry about what I said to Leila. It was wrong."

"And super rude," Wren blurted with a glare.

"Yup. That, too." I nodded. "It's taken me a long time to see it, but . . . Leila's not a nice person. Or a good friend." I paused, then mumbled as a wistful afterthought, "Even if she does love my taste in clothes."

Wren gave a single "Ha!" that bolstered my confidence.

"Anyway, I don't think I'm going to be hanging out with her anymore." I blew out a breath. "I guess I need to work on a lot of things. Like how to be a better friend. A real one." I caught Wren's gaze and held it, making sure she knew I meant it.

An excruciating minute of silence passed, and fear tingled up my spine. What if Wren didn't believe me? Or worse, what if she didn't think I *was* capable of being a good friend?

She stared at her bedspread, but finally said, "You already *are* a good friend, Bria, *when* you quit worrying about what snotty girls like Leila think of you. But that needs to be you *all* the time. Not just some of the time."

"You're right." I moved to sit beside her on her bed. "And I wasn't there for you the way I should've been. I know you've been upset about the sale to CheeseCo, and . . ." I swallowed, dreading that I was about to bring him up *on purpose*, but knowing that I had to. "You kept the whole thing with Gabe under wraps for so long, too. I feel awful I didn't pick up on how you felt about him."

"No." Wren shook her head. "That's partly my fault. I don't exactly walk around with my heart on my sleeve."

I smiled. "Nope. You're pretty much like the sphinx—an emotional enigma."

Now she really laughed. "Maybe I can do better in that department." Then her cheeks reddened. "I . . . actually have some news to share . . . about Gabe. Before he went home tonight, he asked me if I'd go to the movies with him tomorrow."

My pulse quickened, and I stared down at the bedspread to steady myself. I shouldn't have been surprised, especially since I was the one who'd dropped the hint to him in the first place. Still, it was a sharp, vinegar hurt in my heart all the same. I mustered a smile, though, because I didn't want to ruin this moment for Wren. "That's great," I said brightly. "I mean"—I elbowed her—"it's about time, right? You've only had a crush on him since forever."

She laughed and rolled her eyes. "That's true, but I sort of feel like I'm living an alternate reality. I mean, am I *really* going to go on a date with him?"

I pulled her into a hug, glad to see her happy despite the ache inside me. "You are. You can borrow some of my clothes for tomorrow, too, if you want."

She shook her head. "Thanks, but no thanks. Been there, done that." She looked down at her boyfriend jeans and plain tee. "I've decided I'm not going to change who I am for anybody. I'm wearing what I love, no matter what Gabe or anybody else thinks."

"Hey, you never know. You could start a whole new fashion trend. Dungarees could be the next big thing . . ."

Wren burst out laughing. "*Bria*. Don't start."

I laughed. "Okay, okay. Seriously, though, there's a totally different trend I think we should jump on instead." Wren raised a skeptical eyebrow, but I raised my hands to wave off her protests. "*Not* fashion. Dawson's Creamery Crazy Shakes."

Wren frowned. "We're already making new shakes—"

"And we've gotten really good at it." I grabbed the printouts I'd set on my bed and placed them between us. "I checked the sales last night and they've doubled. And then I started thinking about Sip & Shake, the shake place I like in Chicago. It's actually a chain, and they have a ton of shops all over Chicago. It gave me an idea for how we might be able to save the farm from CheeseCo."

Wren's eyes widened. "Okay . . ." she said slowly. "I'm listening."

Pushing thoughts of Gabe aside as best as I could, I explained my idea to Wren. When I finished, there was a new fire in Wren's eyes that hadn't been there earlier. "It's a long shot," she said.

"Mr. Brannigen is coming on Monday to sign the final paperwork with Mom and Dad, and it's next to impossible to change Mom's mind about anything."

"But it's better than no shot at all," I responded. "So . . . ?" I held my breath, waiting.

At last Wren nodded, grinning. "Let's do it. We can look for some old pics of the creamery and Grandpa and Grandma tomorrow, and I'll email the reporter from the *Omaha Gazette* first thing in the morning."

I grinned, too. "And I'll get started on a new shake recipe. Something to knock Mr. Gilford's taste buds into orbit."

We talked for a few more minutes, tossing around shake ideas and possible spots to hang a photo collage in the creamery, and, before I realized what was happening, the awkwardness between us was gone entirely. Soon, we were getting ready for bed, a peaceful quiet settling between us. Thoughts of Gabe still swirled in my head, but they were tempered by thoughts of Wren's excitement over her date with him and our plans for the Fourth of July Bash. Tonight was the first time I'd seen Wren happy since Aunt Beth and Uncle Troy had told her about the farm sale. And doing this for her felt right and good.

Wren flicked off the light and we lay in the darkness, listening to the crickets through the open window. I rolled over and closed my eyes, but not before sending up a wish to the stars that—somehow, some way—my family would get to keep their farm forever.

Chapter Fourteen

I took a sip of ice cold creaminess, but even the gooey, chocolatey goodness of a Smashtastic S'mores shake offered me little comfort. I'd fixed myself the biggest, chocolatiest shake I could and brought it out to the goat pen to drown my misery in marshmallows and Hershey's. Wren and Gabe had left for their date an hour ago, and I'd been absolutely useless ever since.

With the Fourth of July Bash the next day, we'd all been busy. I'd spent most of the day perfecting my new shake recipe and helping Wren unearth photographs and old picture frames from the farmhouse attic. We'd emailed the reporter, Mr. Gilford, and he said that he'd try to stop by the creamery during the celebration.

He was also covering the fireworks show in Omaha, so he couldn't promise that he'd come, but Wren and I still clung to the hope that he might.

Uncle Troy, Luke, and Gabe had decorated the farmyard and barns with red-white-and-blue swags and banners, and Aunt Beth, Wren, and I had decorated the creamery. Even when Aunt Beth decided that we'd hung enough streamers and glitter stars from the ceiling, Wren and I didn't quit. We made sparkling centerpieces out of metallic stars and ribbons and hung a border of red and blue twinkle lights from the sales counter and menu board. We decided we'd wait to hang the photo collage until early Monday morning, as a surprise for Aunt Beth.

For the first time, I'd been truly grateful for Wren's reserved nature. She only brought up Gabe once, and that was only to say that they were leaving for the movies around seven. I could tell by her smile that she was excited, but I was beyond relieved that I didn't have to endure any gushing about him.

After the decorating was done, Wren and Gabe had left for the movie, and now all I could do was obsess over the date I wasn't on.

I took another half-hearted sip of my shake and leaned back against the fence as Tulip nuzzled her head into my shoulder. I lifted my hand to pet her, but instead of accepting my head scratch, she stole a marshmallow from atop my shake instead.

"Hey! *I'm* the one who's stress eating here, you little thief!" I cried with a laugh. "You"—I waggled a scolding finger at her—"are a lousy date."

What were Gabe and Wren doing right this minute? Were they sharing popcorn, or holding hands in the darkened theater? I winced. I didn't want to think about it, but it was all I *could* think about.

"I thought I might find you out here," a voice said, and I turned to see Aunt Beth walking toward the goat pen. She climbed over the fence and sat down beside me. "So . . ." She gently nudged my arm. "How are you?"

"Fine," I lied.

She smiled softly. "Try again." She slid her arm around me, pulling me close. "Honey, there's not much I don't see, and when two girls living under one roof have a crush on the same boy . . ." She chuckled. "Well, that's not all that hard to miss."

"Wren doesn't know," I said quietly.

"I guessed that, too." My aunt nodded.

"I didn't think it was fair to tell her, especially now, when nothing will ever happen between me and Gabe." I sighed. "I want to be happy for her—"

"Of course you do, and I know you're trying." She gave me a squeeze. "I'm so proud of you. You've grown these last few weeks. Your uncle and I both see it, and I've been bragging to your mom and dad about it, too."

"Thanks, Aunt Beth." I gave her a small smile. "But it's hard."

"Putting others first always is." She gave me one more hug. "Come to the house when you're ready. Your uncle and Luke are itching to light some Roman candles out back." She rolled her eyes. "Every year around the Fourth of July, they always get the urge to set things on fire."

I laughed at that, but as soon as she walked away, my restlessness returned. Finally, I gave up on the idea of making peace with Wren and Gabe's date, and turned for the house. If I was going to have a long, agonizing night . . . I figured I might as well set off a few firecrackers.

Very early the next morning, I hammered the last of the photos onto the creamery wall, and then stepped back to view my handiwork. There were now a dozen vintage photos of the Dawson farm and creamery hanging up. There was one of my grandparents standing in front of the creamery's grand opening sign, and another with our entire family—grandparents, parents, and cousins— standing out front. It was taken when Wren, Luke, and I were just toddlers, probably just before my grandparents passed away. The photos told the farm's whole story, and I hoped they would catch people's eyes when they walked through the door.

I was tucking the hammer and nails back under the sales counter when the creamery door opened and Wren walked in, yawning.

"Bria?" She glanced at the photo collage. "Omigosh, you hung them already? They look amazing! But . . . why didn't you wake me up? I was going to help you . . ."

I shrugged. "I was up at four and couldn't sleep anymore after that, so I figured I'd get started." The truth was, I'd barely slept at all. I'd only pretended to be asleep when Wren had tiptoed into the bedroom last night after her date. I hadn't been ready to hear about it yet. I wasn't even sure I was ready to hear about it now, but I knew that at this point, it was as unavoidable as goat pellets. I braced myself and asked, "So . . . how did it go with Gabe last night?"

I held my breath, expecting Wren to burst into an ear-to-ear grin and declare that it was the most incredible night of her life. Instead, she sank into the nearest booth with a grimace.

"The movie was great," she said. "But the date was awful."

I froze, not sure I'd heard her right. "What?"

She laughed, nodding. "Yup. Crazy, right?" She plucked at one of the starry centerpieces, absentmindedly brushing her fingers through its metallic red-and-blue garland. "Turns out that the *idea* of going out with Gabe was nothing like the reality." Her nose wrinkled. "The whole time, I felt like I was hanging out with my brother. It was totally weird."

"Really?" I could scarcely believe it. I felt truly sorry for her, but also tried to push down the zing of relief running through me. "That's . . . too bad."

"It's actually not." She shrugged. "I think I'm just too used to him for him to be a real crush for me. But at least I know that now, and I never have to wonder again."

"So . . . did you tell him that's how you felt?"

She nodded. "He was relieved. He said he felt the same way."

"But . . . but . . ." I shook my head, trying to take it all in as my pulse raced.

"Bria. We only talked about two things the whole night. The movie . . . and you." She grinned at me as my stomach dove to my toes.

"Wh—what?" I stammered.

"I've suspected for a while that *you* were the one Gabe was into. But then you gave me an opening, and I didn't want to admit to myself that Gabe and I are just friends. Until we had such a terrible date."

"Wren, I swear that nothing happened—"

"I know." She held up a hand. "I'm not upset about it. *Really*. I mean, I don't know how you feel about him, but I'm pretty sure he's head over heels for you. And now I know that Gabe and I wouldn't work as a couple anyway."

I shook my head, trying to bring my reeling world back into focus, and sank down into the booth across from her. "So . . . what are you saying?"

Her eyes met mine. "I'm saying that if something ends up happening with you and Gabe . . . I'm okay with it. Got it?" She gave my hand a squeeze.

"Got it," I whispered, but even as I said it, my heart was wrestling with hope and despair. I'd already told Gabe that I didn't like him. How was he ever going to believe anything else I said now? I wanted to rush out to find him, or hide from him for all eternity.

But I didn't have the chance to do either, because at that moment, I heard Aunt Beth calling for us from out in the farmyard. Wren checked the wall clock and stood up decisively.

"We better get ready to open," she said. "Who knows when Mr. Gilford might show up, and CheeseCo's coming at two. If the crowds are going to be as big as I think they are, we're not going to have a spare minute."

I nodded and stood up, too. Right now, I needed to focus on making this the most fantastic Fourth of July this farm had ever seen. And Gabe—sigh—would have to stay an unanswered question.

The crowd that descended on the farm over the next few hours wasn't just big. It was record-breaking. The parking lot was full from the moment the creamery opened, and soon cars were parked on the grass as well. Families flocked to pet the goats and navigate the decorated corn maze. Luke and Gabe were giving hayrides back to back, while Uncle Troy helped in the kitchen. Aunt Beth had created a special Firecracker Burger, complete with hot sauce and pickled jalapeños, and even at ten a.m., burger baskets were flying out of the creamery's kitchen by the dozen.

It didn't feel like any other Fourth I'd ever known. Back in Chicago, Mom and Dad and I would've had a lazy morning together, maybe walking to our favorite corner bakery for breakfast, and then packing up for a day down at Navy Pier, relaxing by the water as we waited for the fireworks. This Fourth of July, between manning the shake station and helping deliver food baskets to customers, I worked nonstop.

Knowing that I had no time to see Gabe was by turns a relief and torture. My tumult of emotions was only compounded by the fact that hour after hour went by without any sign of Mr. Gilford. But then, at one thirty, just as I was losing hope, the reporter appeared, along with Ms. Hale, the photographer we'd seen at the rodeo.

I nudged Wren to get her to glance up from the cash register.

"It's go time," I whispered.

We locked eyes in unspoken understanding and smiled, both of us knowing what we had to do. "Knock his socks off," I said to Wren, and then I hurried to the kitchen to get Aunt Beth while Wren went to greet Mr. Gilford.

"What do you mean, the *Omaha Gazette* is here?" Aunt Beth

gaped as I repeated the news for the second time. "But . . . how? When?"

"We'll tell you later." I grinned. "But right now, you should come out to the dining room. Wren's giving an interview I don't think you want to miss."

Aunt Beth glanced back at Uncle Troy, but he shooed her out of the kitchen. "Go, go! I'll man the kitchen and register. Go!"

We got to the dining room in time to see Wren explaining the photo collage to a rapt Mr. Gilford. "This farm isn't like any other place on earth," Wren was saying. "My grandfather worked as a gas station attendant for years, saving every penny he earned so that he could buy this land. He and my grandmother built the farmhouse, the barns, and this creamery. It took decades."

Mr. Gilford nodded. "And you're the third generation to live and work on this farm," he said. "What makes it special to you?"

"How much time do you have?" Wren joked, then looked around the creamery. "I see myself and my family in everything on our farm—our house, the land, our animals. We don't just raise cows.

We love them. And the land. And this creamery. People who come here for shakes, or hayrides, or the petting zoo . . . they understand that. And they know it makes a difference." She glanced at Aunt Beth. "And that's why I want to take over the farm someday. To keep my family's legacy alive."

Mr. Gilford turned to Aunt Beth. "What do you have to say about your daughter's dream, Mrs. Dawson?"

"I . . . I . . ." Aunt Beth's eyes filled with tears. "I wish her dream could come true, but I'm afraid it can't—"

"It *can*, Mom," Wren said insistently. "You don't have to sell the farm to CheeseCo. Not with the profits we're bringing in from our shakes."

Aunt Beth shook her head, sighing. "Wren—"

"It's true," I piped up. "The website and social media traffic have quadrupled over the last week. Imagine what can happen in another month! Maybe we could even make our shakes in other locations. Like as a milkshake chain," I added before I could lose my nerve.

Aunt Beth's eyes widened. "I had no idea our shakes had made such a difference," she murmured, more to herself than anyone else. "I've been so preoccupied with CheeseCo . . ."

"Look around you, Mom." Wren swept her hand around the dining room while Ms. Hale snapped dozens of pictures. "Almost every single person in here has a shake!"

It was true. Crazy shakes of every color and flavor filled every inch of table space in the room. But Mr. Gilford set his eyes on one shake in particular. He pointed to a red-white-and-blue shake a little boy nearby was slurping down. "What's this shake right here?"

I beamed. "That's our special Fourth of July shake. The Star-Spangled Twizzle Sizzle. Would you like to try one?"

"I'd love to," Mr. Gilford said, and with that, I hurried to the shake machine to get to work. This was the moment I'd been waiting for. The farm's history was Wren's specialty, but the shakes were mine. And if ever there was a moment to make a lasting impression on Mr. Gilford, it was right now.

First, I drizzled strawberry and blueberry syrups down the edges of two shake glasses in alternating columns, then poured in the shake itself: a vanilla shake blended with fresh berries. I squirted huge mountains of whipped cream atop the shakes, and then added red and blue sprinkles, M&M's, and gummy stars. I stuck three Twizzlers into the whipped cream along with a kebob of gummy stars, and then set a red-white-and-blue donut right in the center. Finally, I finished the shakes by sticking a sparking candle into the donut atop each one.

"Hol—y!" Mr. Gilford's mouth dropped open as I set the shakes down on a table in front of him and Ms. Hale. "Those aren't shakes. Those are works of art!"

While Ms. Hale snapped photos of one sparkling shake, Mr. Gilford blew out the candle on his and then dug in, trying to scoop a little bit of everything onto his spoon at once. He took a bite, and sat back chewing and grinning all at once. "That . . ." He swallowed. ". . . is the most overstuffed, oversweetened, over-the-top exercise in excess I've ever tasted!"

"You . . . like it, then?" I asked as my heart thudded.

He beamed. "I *love* it!" And then he was silent for the next few minutes as he finished the shake, down to the very last drop.

When Ms. Hale had finished photographing *her* shake—and downed it, too—she said, "I'd like to get a few photos of the farm facilities, too, if that's all right."

"I'll give you a tour," Wren said quickly, but just as she was about to lead her and Mr. Gilford out into the farmyard, Mr. Brannigen breezed through the creamery door. His CheeseCo partners, plus Luke, were right on his heels.

Luke came straight over to me and Wren. "I saw him pull up," he whispered. "Vulture."

Mr. Brannigen gave Luke a sharp look, as though maybe he'd heard his nickname, but then turned his attention to Aunt Beth.

"Mrs. Dawson," he boomed. Then he paused, taking in Mr. Gilford's and Ms. Hale's press badges. "What's this, now? You've invited the press to cover the sale of the farm to CheeseCo." He smiled. "How perfect!"

"I . . ." Aunt Beth glanced between Mr. Gilford and Mr. Brannigen, and then at Uncle Troy, who walked over from the sales counter to stand beside her.

Wren met Mr. Brannigen's eyes dead-on, standing tall before

him. "The reporters here have nothing to do with CheeseCo. They're interested in *our* farm."

Mr. Brannigen waved a dismissive hand. "Young lady, in a few minutes, it won't be your farm. It will be CheeseCo's."

Wren and Luke looked at Aunt Beth and Uncle Troy pleadingly. "Mom. Dad. Please. Don't," Wren said.

"Aunt Beth." I took her hand. "Do *you* want to keep the farm?"

Everyone seemed to hold their breaths, and even the chatter in the dining room seemed to die down. Mr. Gilford's pen hung suspended over his notepad, his eyes gleaming with the excitement of a great story about to break. Wren and I glanced at each other, and I could see the happy ending she wished for shining in her eyes. *Please*, I thought, *let her wish be granted*.

Aunt Beth stared at the ground for a long minute, and Uncle Troy slid his arm around her shoulders, giving her a fortifying squeeze. "You know," she said softly, "I should've signed the CheeseCo contract days ago, but every time I sit down to do it, I can't bring myself to put the pen to paper. It just doesn't feel right."

At her words, hope rose inside me. I said, "Then look at everything again. See if you can make it work."

She glanced at me. "I didn't think it was so important to you, Bria."

"The farm isn't just a part of Wren and Luke's family history. It's a part of mine, too. It's a special place."

She took my hand. "I've always felt that way about it, and I'm so glad you do, too." She glanced at Uncle Troy, and almost simultaneously, they smiled at each other in some sort of silent understanding. Then Aunt Beth set her shoulders, and turned to Mr. Brannigen. "Mr. Brannigen, there's been a change of plans. We're not selling the farm." She grinned at Wren, Luke, and me in turn, and then did a little dance, whooping. "We're *not* selling the farm!"

There was a burst of jubilant hollering from my entire family as Luke, Wren, and I launched ourselves at Aunt Beth and Uncle Troy for an enormous group hug. As we did, applause and whistles erupted from all over the dining room.

I noticed Mr. Brannigen staring at Aunt Beth and Uncle Troy, seemingly too stunned to speak. "B—but we have a contract!" he finally blustered, waving the CheeseCo papers.

"An *unsigned* contract," Aunt Beth reminded him. "Instead of selling, we'll be looking into franchising opportunities. Our shakes are in high demand. If we can partner with a company interested in investing in our products and sharing in our workload and profits, then maybe we can sell our shakes at other locations. We could start a crazy shake chain, like the girls said."

"This was never discussed in our negotiations." Mr. Brannigen frowned. "CheeseCo's never entertained the idea of franchises."

"Until now." Wren stepped forward. "You like uncovering opportunities in surprising places, right?"

"Y-yes, I suppose I do . . ." He fiddled with the papers in his hands.

"Then I'm sure you'll want to be the first one to see the business proposal my parents are going to put together, before they shop it around to other companies."

Mr. Brannigen glanced at his partners, and there was a subtle but collective nodding of heads. He cleared his throat gruffly. "Yes. Yes, I'd like that." He smoothed the lapels of his jacket. "Well. If we're not signing contracts today, there's only one thing left to do."

"What's that, Mr. Brannigen?" Luke asked.

He smiled. "Enjoy one of those shakes of yours."

Wren and I shared wide grins.

"Coming right up," I said.

Wren turned to Mr. Gilford. "I'd be happy to give you that tour of the rest of the farm, if you still want to write about us in your article."

"An up-and-coming future farmer like you? Oh, you can bet I'm going to write about you." Mr. Gilford slipped his notebook into his pants pocket. "Family-run businesses like this are few and far between, so don't be surprised if your farm gets the spotlight. I expect the feature to run toward the end of this week, but I'll let you know the exact date."

As Wren, Mr. Gilford, and Ms. Hale made their way out the door, I went back to the shake machine, smiling. Still, the happiness I felt over my family's victory was tinged with a bittersweet regret. The one other person I wanted to celebrate this moment with was Gabe. But the only glimpse I'd had of him all day long was on his tractor in the distance. As the door swung closed, I could hear the tractor's faraway rumble, and my heart tugged in my chest. I wanted to fly after the sound.

But what would be the use of that? Gabe probably didn't want to see me, or speak to me. Not after I'd turned him down. No. I needed to stay here, and so did my heart, in this moment, celebrating with my family. And Gabe?

I sighed wistfully. Gabe would be my one summer regret.

By the time Mr. Brannigen and his CheeseCo partners left, the afternoon had turned into evening. Mr. Brannigen had devoured not one, but two Star-Spangled Twizzle Sizzles, and then had gone back to the house to talk shake franchising possibilities with Aunt Beth and Uncle Troy. I didn't know how the meeting had gone, but I had a good feeling about it. After all, nobody drank two crazy shakes without *really* loving them. That much was certain. And if he loved them, maybe it meant he'd come to love this new idea about a shake chain, too.

After we closed up the creamery for the night, Wren, Luke, and my aunt and uncle decided to head down to the pond for swimming and fireworks. While Uncle Troy and Luke finished the evening's milking, Aunt Beth, Wren, and I packed burgers into a picnic basket in the kitchen.

"You're coming to the pond, right?" Wren asked me. "No leeches this time. Promise."

I smiled. "I'll be down in a while," I said. I needed to be alone with my thoughts for a few minutes, to let go of the last bit of hope I'd clung to all day. I'd seen the tractor parked in the farmyard earlier, and there was no sign of Gabe anywhere. He'd gone home, without a single word to me.

Aunt Beth turned to me with a warm hug. "I still can't believe what you and Wren pulled off today. My girls, standing up to Mr. Brannigen." She shook her head, grinning at both of us. "I guess I better get busy looking into franchises now."

"And we have more crazy shakes to invent this summer," I said with a glance at Wren, who nodded. "*And* . . . maybe more rodeos to attend?" I asked hopefully.

Aunt Beth and Wren exchanged glances and laughed.

"Honey, if you want another rodeo," Aunt Beth said, "you'll *get* another rodeo."

"Look out. We've created a monster." Wren elbowed me. "Next you'll want to go night fishing again, too."

"Maybe. Who knows?" I shrugged. "There's tons I want to do the rest of the summer. I have my sketchbook to fill with new shakes, and maybe some other drawings, too. I'll need to practice, because when I get back to school, I want to sign up for art, and maybe a graphic design class, too."

"You certainly have an eye for it," my aunt said.

I grinned. "But while I'm here, I want to make the most of the farm, dirt and all." I paused. "Aunt Beth? I've been thinking . . . could I come to stay again? Maybe next summer?"

Aunt Beth beamed and hugged me again. "Oh, honey, we'd love that so much."

Wren glanced over her shoulder at me as we walked out the creamery's door. "Only next time, bring your own work boots."

I stuck out my tongue at her, laughing, and then waved as she and my aunt walked toward the pond.

I headed for the red barn and the old tire swing, feeling the need for its tried-and-true comfort. I climbed on, pushing off with one leg to set it in motion. I tilted my head back and closed my eyes, feeling the dipping and diving, and the warm evening air streaming across my face. I wouldn't think about Gabe anymore, I told myself. Instead, I'd think about the email I'd gotten back from Jane this afternoon—the one thanking me for my apology and saying I could call her when I got back to Chicago and *maybe* we'd grab a shake together. I'd think about all the ways I could start the school year by being a better friend to her and Devany. I'd think about what I could do with my love for design, and all the fun ways I could turn that into a creative job someday. Most of all, I'd think about how this barn and this swing—and the entire Dawson family farm—would be here for years and years more, and that, in my own little way, I'd helped make that happen.

I lost track of time, caught in the easy swooping rhythm of the swing, and soon the sky beyond the barn door had purpled into dusk. I might have stayed like that, swinging my thoughts of Gabe away forever, if warm hands hadn't caught me about the waist, slowly easing the swing to a stop.

"Gabe?" I breathed as he turned the swing around. Then I was looking into his gray eyes, our faces inches from each other. "I—I thought you went home already."

"I had to talk to you. To tell you how sorry I was. All those things I said . . ." He shook his head. "I was way out of line—"

"No, *I* was the one out of line." I sucked in a breath. "The thing is . . . I lied. I told you that I didn't like you, but it wasn't true. I knew Wren was crushing on you, and I couldn't hurt her." The words came out in a rush.

"Oh." Gabe's eyes lit up, and he nodded slowly. "I understand," he said. "I wouldn't have wanted to hurt her, either." He passed a hand over his hair. "But now she knows it wouldn't have worked. We both do. And it's all good."

"I just wish I'd never lied to you," I said softly. My heart clanged wildly against my ribs, with wondering and fresh hope. "Because you're the first real crush I ever had. The only one."

"You are, too," Gabe whispered, and my face burned with happiness. Then he smiled. "You *do* know how to shake things up, Bria Muller. I'll give you that."

I grinned "Ha! Very *punny*. But just so you know, you turned my world upside down, too, Mr. Dark Side of the Spoon."

He shrugged, laughing. "I have my moments." He leaned down to pick up a tall glass from the ground. "Here. I made this for you."

I laughed, staring down at the shake he held in his hands. Swimming in the thick vanilla shake were mini chocolate cows, and decorating the edge of the glass were more chocolate animals— cows, pigs, horses, and goats.

"Whoa," I said, impressed. "What sort of a crazy shake is *that*?"

He tilted his head. "How about a . . . Second Chance Shake?"

"Would that mean a second chance for the farm? Or for you?"

He blushed. "Maybe . . . both?"

"And maybe for me, too," I said. "Thank you." I took a sip. The shake wasn't as expertly made as one Wren or I would have concocted, but it was delicious all the same.

Just then, a starburst of fiery red and blue exploded in the night sky beyond the barn doors.

"The fireworks are starting," Gabe said.

Together we lifted our eyes to the sky, taking in the spectacular show. As showers of gold sparks rained down like magic fairy dust, Gabe's hand found mine. The moment our fingertips touched, the electric warmth made me feel like I was floating up into the sky, my heart as bright as the lights bursting above.

"Not too shabby for a small-town fireworks show, right?" Gabe whispered when the show ended.

I shrugged. "Meh," I said with feigned indifference. "I don't know. I was expecting a much bigger finale."

"Wha—? A bigger finale," he mumbled under his breath. Then, louder and in disbelief. "A bigger finale!"

I giggled, and he grabbed me around the waist teasingly, but then I lost my breath entirely when, in the moonlight, I saw his face inches from mine, stars flecked in his eyes. "Bria," he whispered, and my heart flared like a big fireworks finale at the way he said my name.

Time seemed to slow as I looked into his eyes. "Do you remember when I first came here? You told me you hoped I'd find a reason to change my mind about the farm."

"I remember," he said quietly.

"I found a lot of good reasons," I whispered, "and one really great one." I smiled up at him. "You."

He smiled back slowly, brushing a strand of hair from my forehead, and leaned toward me. Our lips met in a soft touch that swept the earth, the stars, and the entire universe away, until it felt like just the two of us, spinning through delicious space.

"If I'm your first crush, does that mean that was your first kiss?" he whispered when our lips parted.

"Yes," I breathed as my heart thrilled. "But hopefully not the last?"

He smiled once more. "We have all summer." Our lips met again in a perfect blend of impossible sweetness, better than any shake in the world.

Dawson's Creamery
Crazy Shake Recipes

Are you ready for a taste of frosty sweetness?

Give some of Bria's crazy shake recipes a try,

and you'll be chillin' in no time! To make any

of these shakes, you'll need a blender or food

processor. Just remember to always use adult

supervision when you're using a blender, and

never open a blender lid or put anything

into a blender while it's running.

Shake-Making Basics

For each shake, you'll need: a glass mug or mason jar, 2 to 3 wooden or plastic skewers, a straw, and a blender.

The key to making any crazy shake is accessorizing your glass mug *before* you blend your shake. First, drizzle chocolate sauce around the edge of a glass mug, coating the edge and the top of the mug. It's okay if it drips into the inside of the mug and down the side; overflowing fudge sauce will make your shake look even more scrumptious. Put the mug in the freezer for 1 to 2 minutes. Then, remove the mug from the freezer. Now the fun starts. Using the ingredients in each recipe, press some of your extras—sprinkles, crumbled cookie, candy bar bits—into the sauce along the outside of the glass. You have to be quick! As soon as you're happy with your decorating, put the mug back in the freezer and leave it there while you make the rest of the shake.

Next, you can prepare your skewers, which you should load up with the most delicious, and most eye-catching, ingredients from the recipe. Have fun and get creative! Once the skewers are full, set them aside.

Now it's time to blend your shake! Mix on "frozen drink" setting until fully blended. After grabbing your mug from the freezer, pour the shake into it. Top the shake with a heaping mountain of whipped cream (you could use homemade, Reddi-wip, or Cool Whip) and garnish it with more sprinkles or candy pieces. Lastly, stick your decorated skewers into your shake, add a straw, and enjoy! Each recipe below suggests some flavor combos, but remember that there's always room for accessorizing and experimenting.

Maniacal Mudslide

Ingredients for the shake:

2–3 scoops chocolate ice cream

½ cup ice-cold milk

½ cup brownie chunks (you can bake everything-but-the-kitchen-sink brownies, complete with pretzel bits, toffee bits, and dark and white chocolate morsels, but a plain brownie works perfectly as well)

Ingredients for accessorizing the shake:

¼–½ cup fudge sauce or ganache (for the edge of the glass)

Chocolate sprinkles

¼ cup toffee bits

7–8 mini marshmallows

¼ cup pretzel bits

2–3 caramel squares

Handful of plain or caramel popcorn

3–4 Oreo cookies

1 brownie square

Whipped cream

Directions:

Prepare your glass mug as described on page 254. Once the fudge sauce is ready to be decorated, cover it with sprinkles and toffee bits. You can stick mini marshmallows, pretzel bits, caramel squares, or popcorn into the sauce as well. Next, stack your skewers with alternating marshmallows, Oreos, and caramels. Be sure to include one big brownie square on one skewer as well.

To make your shake, place 2 to 3 heaping scoops of chocolate ice cream in your blender. Pour in the milk and add the brownie chunks.
Blend it up, pour it into your glass, and
start decorating! Don't forget to add plenty
of whipped cream. Add a straw and enjoy!

The Dark Side of the Spoon

Ingredients for the shake:

2–3 scoops mint chocolate chip ice cream

½ cup ice-cold milk

3–4 York Peppermint Patties, broken into pieces

Ingredients for accessorizing the shake:

¼–½ cup fudge sauce or ganache (for the edge of the glass)

Chocolate sprinkles

Handful of semisweet chocolate chips

5–8 Junior Mints

3–4 York Peppermint Patties

1–2 peppermint sticks

Whipped cream

Directions:

Once the fudge sauce is ready to be decorated, cover it with sprinkles and chocolate chips. On your skewers, alternate Junior Mints and Peppermint Patties. Blend up your shake ingredients, add the skewers and peppermint sticks, and top your whipped cream with any leftover chocolate chips and candies. Delicious!

Twixie Tornado

Ingredients for the shake:

2–3 scoops vanilla ice cream

½ cup ice-cold milk

4 mini Heath bars

2 Twix bars

Ingredients for accessorizing the shake:

¼–½ cup fudge sauce or ganache (for the edge of the glass)

Heath toffee bits

Rainbow sprinkles

Chunks of cut-up Twix bars and mini Heath bars

1–2 chocolate chip cookies

Whipped cream

Directions:

Cover the edges of the glass with toffee bits and rainbow sprinkles using your fudge sauce. You can add chunks of cut-up Twix or Heath bar as well. Prepare your skewers with alternating Twix and Heath bar chunks, or add pieces of cookies. Mix up the vanilla ice cream and milk with more Heath and Twix bars, and accessorize with whipped cream, skewers, and the rest of the toffee bits and sprinkles. Set a chocolate chip cookie on top, and enjoy!

Star-Spangled Twizzle Sizzle

Ingredients for the shake:

2–3 scoops strawberry, blackberry, raspberry, or cherry

ice cream

½ cup ice-cold milk

Ingredients for accessorizing the shake:

¼ cup strawberry, or any other kind of berry, sauce (for

the edge of the glass)

Red, white, and blue sprinkles, plus any red-white-

and-blue or star-shaped candies you want to add

2–3 red Twizzlers, one cut into pieces

½ cup fresh strawberries, blackberries, and blueberries

Whipped cream

A patriotic donut

A sparkling candle (optional)

Directions:

Instead of fudge sauce, use berry sauce to adorn your glass with sprinkles and bits of Twizzler. Your skewers can get festive with berries and Twizzler pieces. Top your berry shake base with a peak of whipped cream, plus more sprinkles, patriotic candies, berries, and Twizzlers. Leave space for a whole donut on top, as well as your skewers. For extra pizzazz, carefully stick a sparkling candle right into the donut— and enjoy!

More Delicious Treats from
Suzanne Nelson

Find more reads
you will love . . .

When Sam discovers two mystery pugs left on her porch, she knows her parents won't be happy . . . But she *has* to take in the abandoned pups. Only, she's not quite prepared for how hard it is to hide the frisky duo. Thankfully, cute new boy in town, Jai, is down to help. But if the dogs' original owner comes forward, will Sam have to give up the pugs she's fallen in love with?

Have you read all the (wish) books?

- ☐ *Clementine for Christmas* by Daphne Benedis-Grab
- ☐ *Carols and Crushes* by Natalie Blitt
- ☐ *Allie, First at Last* by Angela Cervantes
- ☐ *Gaby, Lost and Found* by Angela Cervantes
- ☐ *Sit, Stay, Love* by J. J. Howard
- ☐ *Pugs and Kisses* by J. J. Howard
- ☐ *Pugs in a Blanket* by J. J. Howard
- ☐ *The Boy Project* by Kami Kinard
- ☐ *Best Friend Next Door* by Carolyn Mackler
- ☐ *11 Birthdays* by Wendy Mass
- ☐ *Finally* by Wendy Mass
- ☐ *13 Gifts* by Wendy Mass
- ☐ *The Last Present* by Wendy Mass
- ☐ *Graceful* by Wendy Mass
- ☐ *Twice Upon a Time: Beauty and the Beast, the Only One Who Didn't Run Away* by Wendy Mass
- ☐ *Twice Upon a Time: Rapunzel, the One with All the Hair* by Wendy Mass
- ☐ *Twice Upon a Time: Sleeping Beauty, the One Who Took a Really Long Nap* by Wendy Mass

☐ *Blizzard Besties* by Yamile Saied Méndez

☐ *Playing Cupid* by Jenny Meyerhoff

☐ *Cake Pop Crush* by Suzanne Nelson

☐ *Macarons at Midnight* by Suzanne Nelson

☐ *Hot Cocoa Hearts* by Suzanne Nelson

☐ *You're Bacon Me Crazy* by Suzanne Nelson

☐ *Donut Go Breaking My Heart* by Suzanne Nelson

☐ *Sundae My Prince Will Come* by Suzanne Nelson

☐ *I Only Have Pies for You* by Suzanne Nelson

☐ *Shake It Off* by Suzanne Nelson

☐ *Confectionately Yours: Save the Cupcake!* by Lisa Papademetriou

☐ *My Secret Guide to Paris* by Lisa Schroeder

☐ *Sealed with a Secret* by Lisa Schroeder

☐ *Switched at Birthday* by Natalie Standiford

☐ *The Only Girl in School* by Natalie Standiford

☐ *Once Upon a Cruise* by Anna Staniszewski

☐ *Deep Down Popular* by Phoebe Stone

☐ *Revenge of the Flower Girls* by Jennifer Ziegler

☐ *Revenge of the Angels* by Jennifer Ziegler